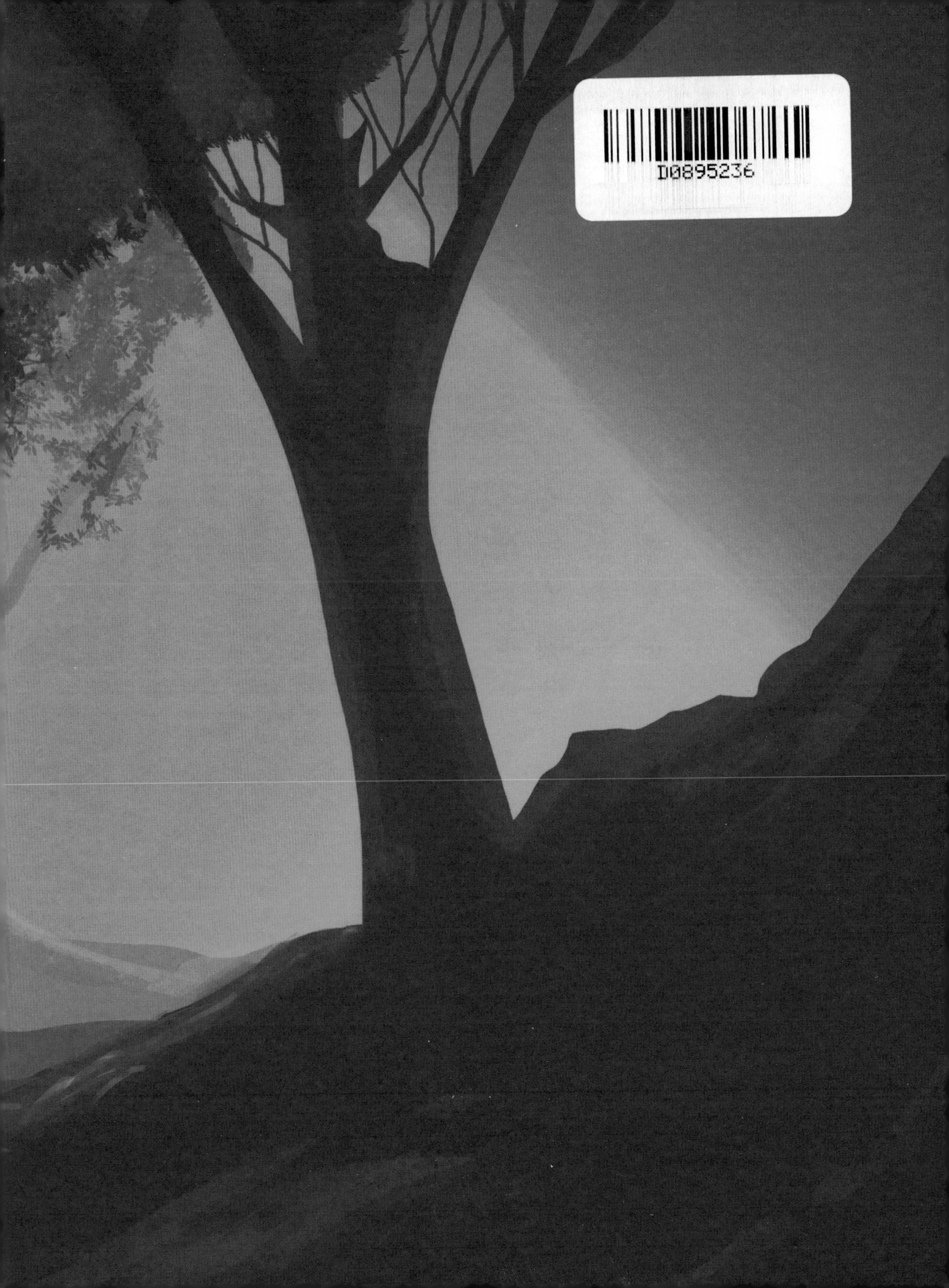

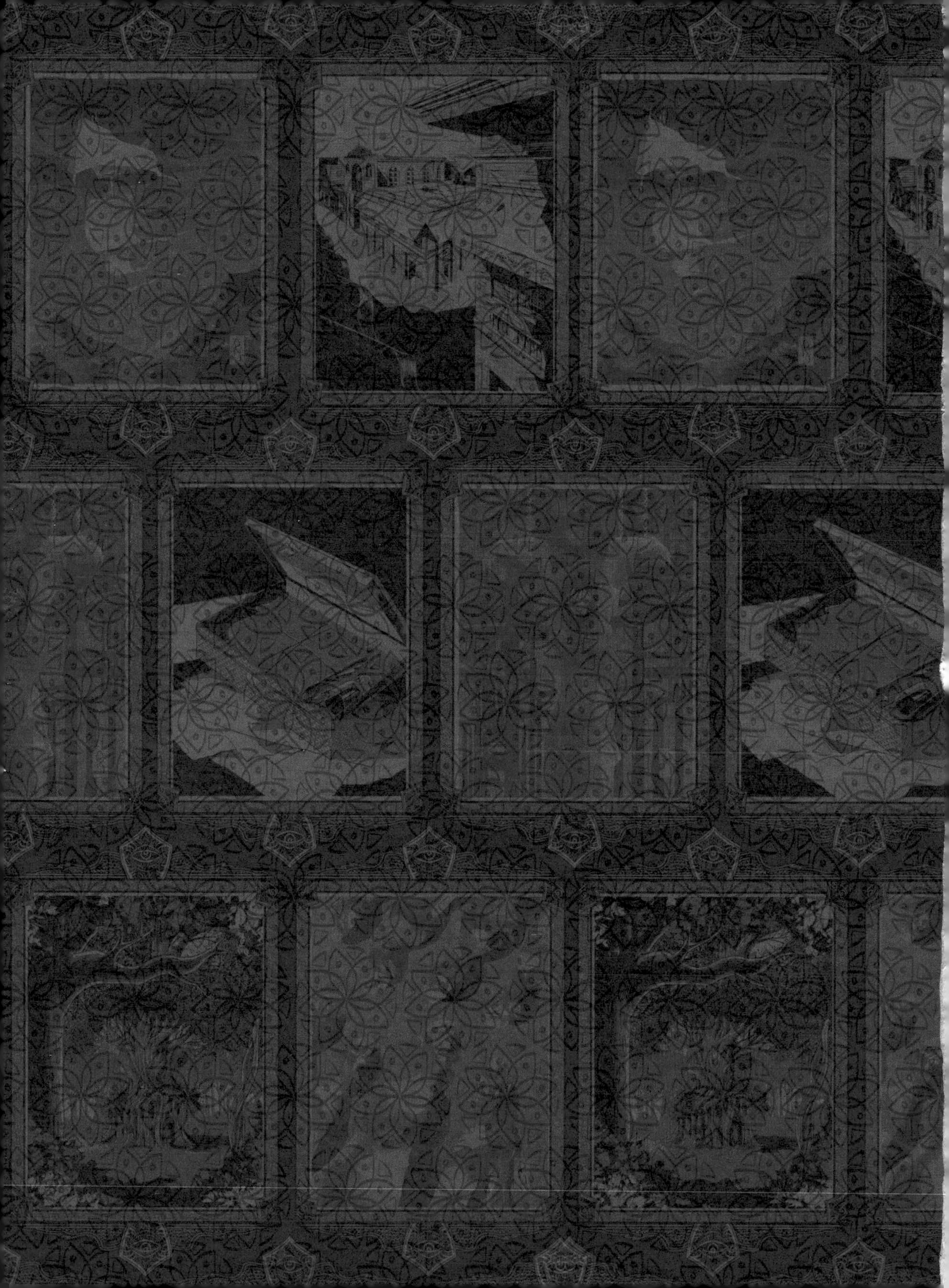

THE BLACK BESTIARY

A Phantasmagoria of Monsters and Myths from the Philippines

David Hontiveros · Budjette Tan
Kajo Baldisimo · Bow Guerrero · Mervin Malonzo

TUTTLE Publishing

Tokyo | Rutland, Vermont | Singapore

TABLE OF CONTENTS

KIBAAN
– 45 –

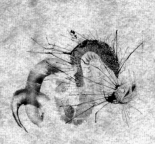

MAMELEU
– 55 –

MANTIW
– 69 –

TAHAMALING
– 71 –

TIBURONES
– 113 –

TIKTIK
– 115 –

TO MY ESTEEMED COLLEAGUES

Before anything else, let me say this:

There has still been no sign whatsoever of my former colleague. He is still officially considered "Missing," and his family has offered up a substantial reward for any information regarding his whereabouts.

They have also roundly denounced my "unfair" characterization of him in *The Lost Journal* (which I will hereafter refer to as the "LJ").

I'm writing this piece in a secret location. I know where I am, of course, but no one else does, not even our publisher.

I find myself here today because of the ever-escalating sense of paranoia and fear that gripped me as we wrapped up the LJ.

I lived those days shrouded in dread, wondering when I would answer the phone or the doorbell, and that my former colleague had finally decided to silence me, and had brought his new friends with him so I could make their fatal acquaintance.

Ultimately, it came down to a number of the experts we had brought in on the LJ. Once they saw how serious I was with my intentions for the LJ, and how anxiety was slowly but surely getting the better of me, they made a suggestion.

And I took them up on it.

Now, you know those compounds deep in the woods or up in the mountains, the ones run by a bunch of wackadoo survivalists who've hunkered down with guns and ammo and supplies, just waiting for the inevitable breakdown of society? (Take your pick of apocalypse: nuclear, viral, or zombie?)

Well, *that's* the kind of place where I am now.

Though perhaps the term "wackadoo" is a bit harsh. (We also may or may not be located deep in the woods or up in the mountains; anyone who's read the LJ knows that most of these creatures consider the wilderness *their* territory…)

While living in this kind of environment took some getting used to, I have to admit that I'm not scared anymore, not like before.

And it's not simply because these people know it really is about being *prepared* for a possible supranatural apocalypse, *just in case.*

It's also about being around people who know what I know now, who know about the nature of the darkness that's out there, waiting to swallow the unsuspecting and the ignorant.

It was from the safety of this new living space that I appreciated the modest success that greeted the LJ. It didn't burn up the charts the way some other titles dubiously do, but it made enough of an impact that our publisher decided to take us out for another spin.

This, in and of itself, was a surprise, but I have to admit, the biggest surprise—and the one I hadn't really anticipated—was the amount of people around the world who claim to have had encounters with the supranatural.

Our publisher was *deluged* with letters and documents and *manuscripts*, all claiming one kind of odd and true encounter or another.

I've gone through every single one of those accounts, and yes, some of them are most *definitely* wackadoo (and here, I do not feel guilty for using the term, not in the slightest), while some are decidedly *not* true.

Some ripped off the plots of Asian horror movies wholesale, others were told in the third person for no apparent reason, at least one was written in screenplay format, while another was a lurid bit of erotica (in which the apparent victim turns the tables on the creature of the night that is stalking her and becomes his dominant mistress), and yet another was presented as an elevator pitch, with the promise of more forthcoming, should we be "interested" in the story.

So while some of these accounts were in direct opposition to our stand in the LJ, of presenting the *truth*, others could not be so easily dismissed.

Some required deep research and verification, wave after wave of scrutiny and fact-checking, until I was satisfied that the account was, to the best of our knowledge, true.

And among those accounts that passed my barrage of litmus tests was a very pivotal one, that became central to this follow-up to the LJ.

Once our publisher made the decision to jump back into these waters, we arrived at an agreement regarding the structure of this follow-up.

While our publisher wanted to burn through the work that my former colleague had written (largely creature entries which had not been included in the LJ), they were also interested in taking advantage of all the accounts that had been sent their way.

So this follow-up to the LJ, while continuing the threads of the original, is going to look different.

There are still some creature entries, but there will also be a number of first-person accounts, vetted by me, as well as journal entries from a contemporary of Alejandro Pardo, and a few other odds and ends.

While the creature entries herein are all written by my former colleague, pre-disappearance, I was kept busy with vetting the accounts we chose to present here. I also helped organize all the other material that this book contains, and wrote all the other text pieces herein.

As with the LJ, to preserve the anonymity of all concerned, any names mentioned here are fictitious (as are the bios of the creative team, which now includes amongst its ranks a number of new artists brought on board by our publisher).*

We should probably leave it at that for the time being.

For now, let me once again invite you through this strange door, into the world of darkness and shadows that Alejandro Pardo has helped shed a light on…

*Though with the high visibility of my former colleague's family's ongoing search, it will not take Sherlock Holmes to uncover my identity. But, as per our publisher's wishes, we maintain the pseudonymous illusion.

FIRST-HAND ACCOUNTS
OF THE SUPRANATURAL

My vetting process for the accounts* we received was as exhausting as I could make it. It was arduous, but also necessary, if I was to maintain the stringent standards for the truth that we established in the LJ.

One of the later stages of the vetting process involved requesting the individual who had sent the account (the "witness," as we would come to call them) to narrate it back to me.

    This was, of course, another layer of verification: Any narrated accounts that were too similar to the original written ones—those where there weren't any noticeable differences in word choice and phrasing, that sounded like they'd been memorized or rehearsed—were summarily discarded.

These sessions were recorded, and those recordings provided the basis for the first-person accounts published herein.

    What you will be reading here are transcripts of those sessions. They are largely verbatim, and edits were made only in the interest of space and clarity and instances of coarse language.

    To the best of our determination, these accounts are as true as their witnesses claim them to be.

    Additionally, all illustrations found in this section are artistic interpretations based on the witnesses' accounts.

---

* Since the accounts came from all over the globe, there were several that, even after passing my thorough vetting process, concerned creatures that had no direct counterparts or similarities with those of our local folklore.

    As such, those particular accounts did not make a good fit for this follow-up to the LJ. Our publisher, however, is keenly interested in making use of those accounts, and we may yet see those in a future publication.

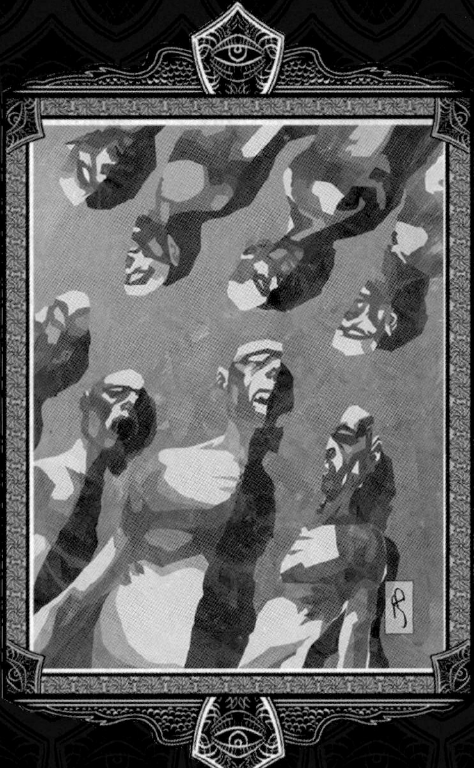

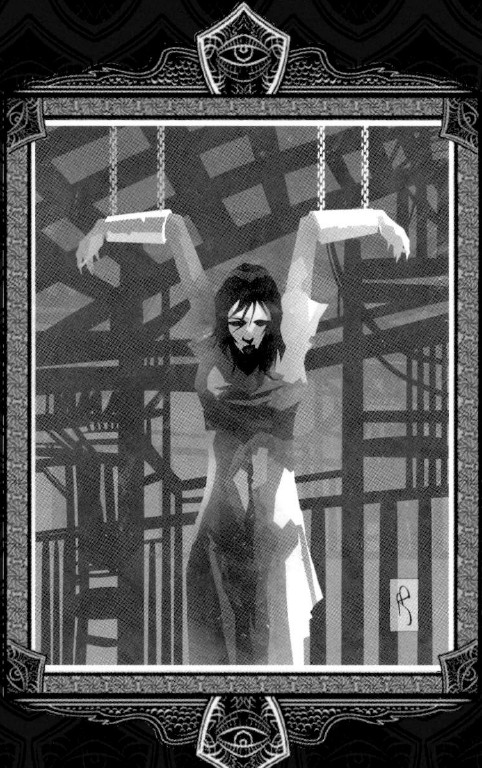

R.J.
WE'RE YOUR DEMONS

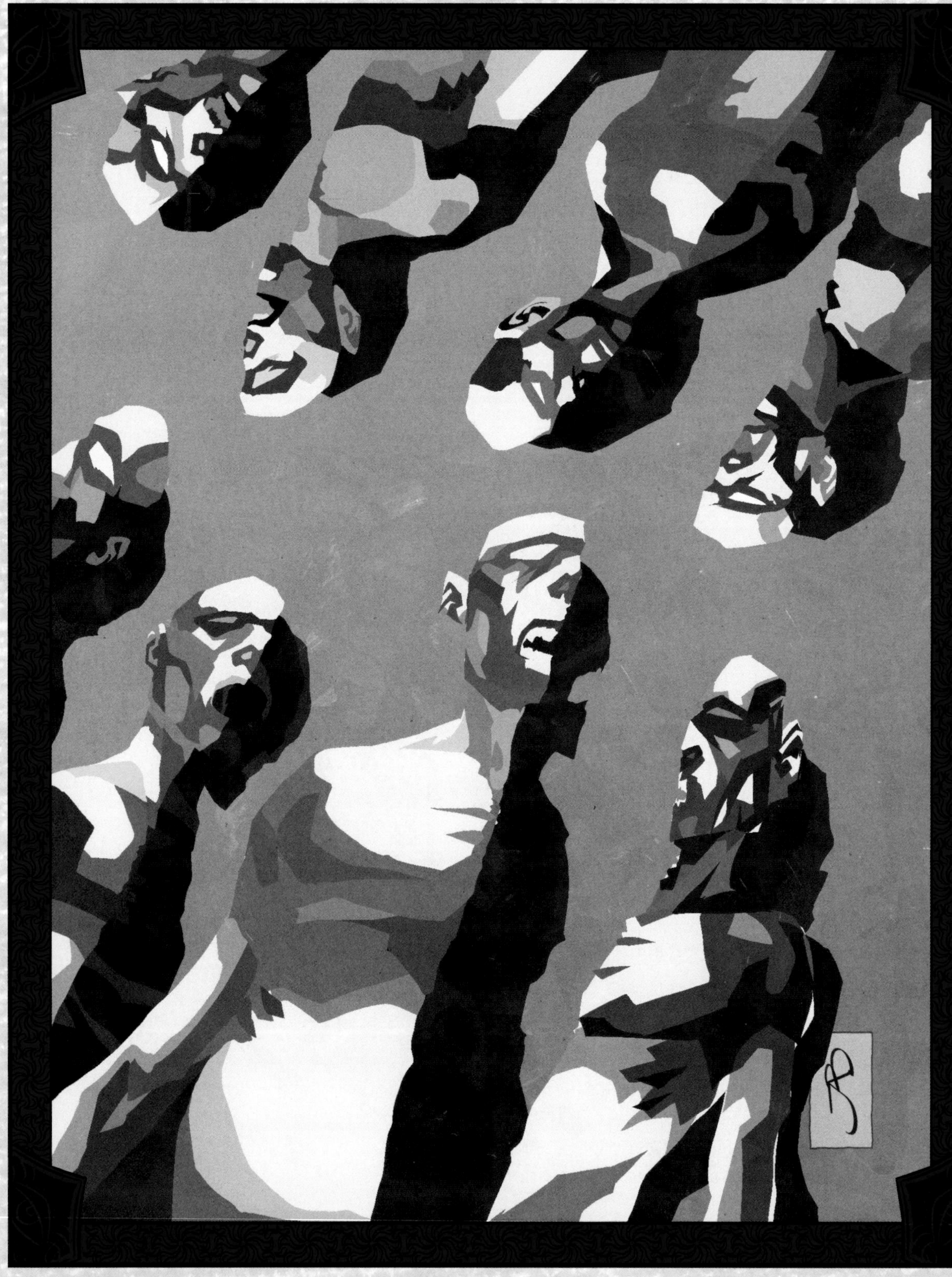

My name's Josephine, but friends call me "R.J."

I used to be a civil servant, an employee of the United States government.

I worked for one of the acronyms.

But you won't find any record of me ever being one of them, not if they did their jobs right.

After everything went down, my whole *life* as one of them was redacted, years of distinguished and exemplary service—including my prior military background—scrubbed by people who'd rather bury their heads in the sand than accept that there's a whole lot of things in the world that they can't even *begin* to explain.

Which I realize won't make your verification process any easier, but it's *another* organization that's vouching for me now, right?

So… let's start at the beginning.

Like so many other stories, this one starts when a boy meets a girl.

Except when that happened, it wasn't my story yet. It was my *brother's*.

Tony met Allison at a Starbucks, and they hit it off instantly. I met Allison for the first time at my father's birthday party, when Tony brought her home to meet our parents.

A few months after that, they both went missing. Three days after, Tony's mutilated corpse was found in Rocheport, Missouri.

He had been pumped full of iron buckshot from a 10-gauge shotgun. His body had then been flash-frozen and sliced in half—vertically, down the spine—by an industrial-grade, electric meat saw. One half was hastily buried on one bank of the Missouri River, the other half buried on the opposite bank.

Those kinds of details would ring alarm bells in anyone who's seen *The Lost Journal*, but your book was still years away from publication.

What we had back then was a gruesome murder case, with an M.O. that matched a handful of cases down over the years, all of which had turned into investigative dead ends.

Tony's case quickly became more of the same. One dead end after another. The only promising lead was Allison and no one was sure whether she was another victim, or the perpetrator.

I wasn't officially on the case of course, given my connection to the victim, but that didn't stop me. I insinuated my way onto the case any chance I got, and truthfully, "insinuate" is a very nice word for what it was I was doing.

But there just wasn't anything there, and there was no sign of Allison anywhere.

The case was going nowhere.

Until the bodies were found in India.

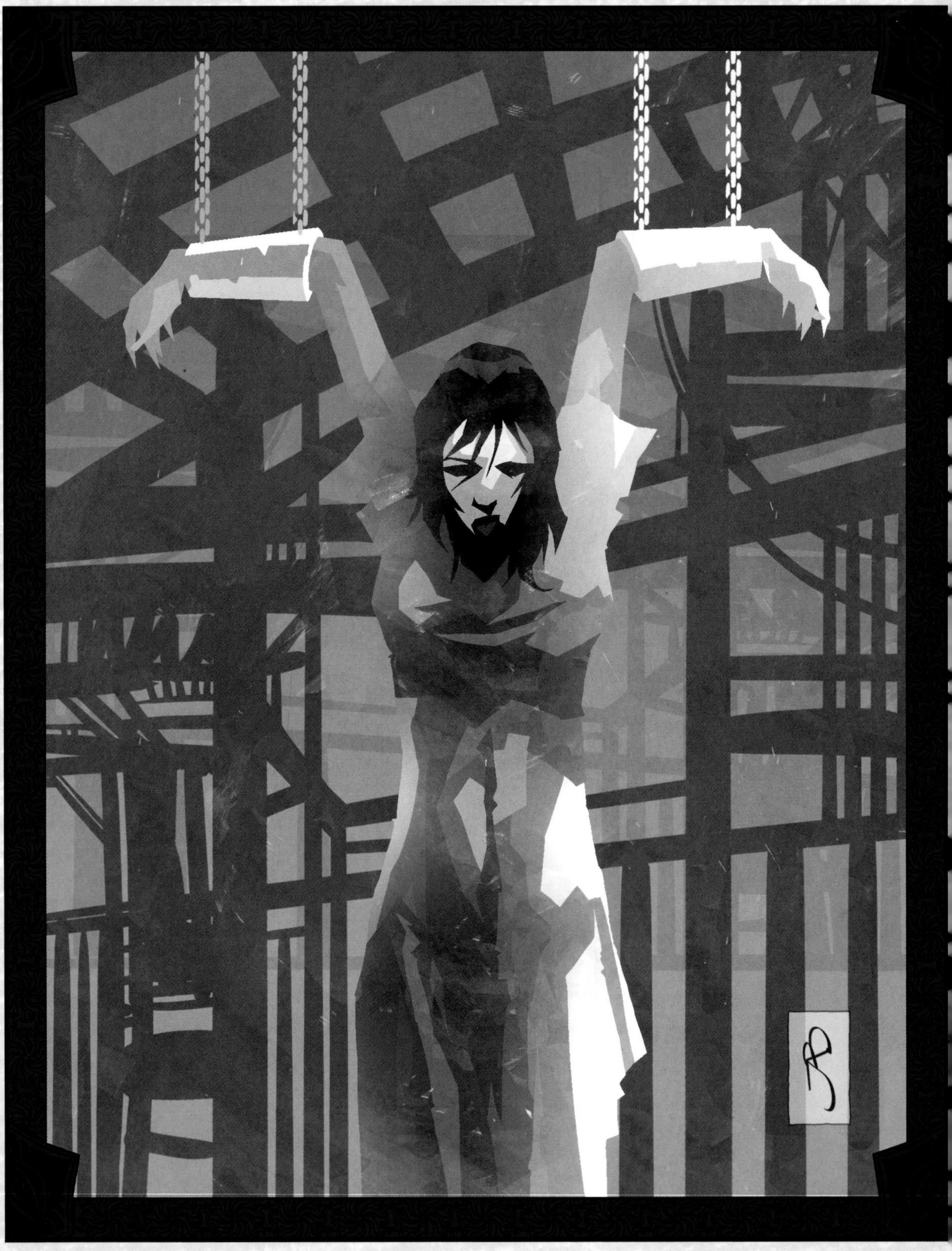

Monsoon season in India had been particularly bad that year, and the flooding had been catastrophic.

But it also caused a whole lot of upheaval along the country's various river banks. A number of mutilated corpses were found, some halves not even matching up with any others found. They estimated the remains found came from a dozen victims, in varying stages of decomposition.

The authorities were kept busy with the flooding, of course, so there wasn't any immediacy to investigating the remains, especially since none seemed to be recent deaths.

But the details of the mutilations couldn't be ignored.

So I took some leave, went down to India, and effectively flushed my career down the crapper.

India was a *nightmare.*

If my drive to find Tony's killer was inconvenient for some suits back home, it was *apocalyptic* in India.

I threw my weight around, flashing my acronymed credentials at the slightest provocation (even though I wasn't there on any kind of official business and I was way out of my jurisdiction). Not to mention the fact that India isn't exactly the most forward-thinking country when it comes to women, let alone *foreign* women in authority.

I was off the rails. I'd gone rogue.

But I didn't give a good goddamn. I was gonna find Tony's killer, and if I had to burn down my career to do that, then that's exactly what I was gonna do.

And then I saw Allison.

And then I met my brother's killer.

I was on Sudder Street, making a crucial decision about where to have dinner (it's always Russian roulette when my stomach meets unfamiliar cuisine), when who do I spot tailing me but Allison.

And two things hit me at once.

One: She's done this before. She isn't quite professional level, but this isn't anything new to her. I might not even have noticed her, if I'd been a civilian.

Two: This is not the down-home girl Allison I met at my Dad's birthday party. This is a *colder* Allison. A more focused Allison.

Those two things led me to this realization: I needed to have a good talk with this girl.

So I decided to lure her to the one place in this foreign country that I was familiar and intimate with: my hotel room.

I'd memorized its layout, its dimensions, I knew where everything was and how to maneuver effectively within its perimeter. It was the closest thing to home turf I was gonna get, so I wasn't about to waste that advantage.

So I told my stomach to wait a bit longer, and I walked back to the hotel, making sure Allison was still tailing me.

Of course, when I got back to my room, someone was already there, waiting for me.

Waiting for *us*.

I hadn't even turned on the lights and shut the door behind me when there was a quick sting at the side of my neck.

And I was out cold.

I woke up in some dingy warehouse, tied to a chair, my head still pounding from the drug they'd dosed me with.

Allison was a few feet in front of me, hung from the rafters by her manacled wrists.

And she was awake.

The first word out of her mouth, and I thought, *This is the down-home girl Allison I met at Dad's party. This is not the one that had been tailing me down Sudder Street.*

She was scared, she said. She didn't know what was happening, she said. She didn't know how she got here, she said.

I'm not really sure what I would have done just then; whether I was gonna call her out and tell her I'd seen her on Sudder Street, or if I was gonna play along and see where that got me.

I hadn't made my decision yet, when the people waiting for me in my hotel room chose to show their hand.

Have you seen one, up close? An *aswang*?

It isn't pretty, I can tell you that.

They told me. *Everything.*

They *showed* me. Showed me what Allison *really* looked like.

Allison was an *aswang*. She was in Kolkata because of me. And they were in Kolkata because of her.

Allison was an *aswang*, and she'd *turned* my brother into one. They'd had to *kill* my brother, like they'd killed so many others over the years.

They killed Allison right in front of me.

To *show* me.

So I could *learn*.

Afterwards, after I'd joined their ranks, they showed me files. They showed me the things you needed to *look* for.

And I saw them.

I saw them in my brother's autopsy report.

His mutilated remains showed signs of severe iron deficiency.

That's one of the signs of an *aswang*, when a CBC *[complete blood count-Eds.]* indicates iron deficiency anemia, but the patient displays none of the usual symptoms.

I was shown medical reports of people whose red blood cells weren't carrying enough oxygen to their body's tissues. Technically, these people should have been dead, but somehow, that thing, the black chick, it was keeping them alive.

They also told me, later on, that they could have tried to cure Tony, to extract the black chick, but he'd been in a frenzy, and he'd given them no choice but to take him down the way they had.

I told them I understood.

I told them that they did the right thing.

Because even if they'd managed to take that damned thing out of him, even if they'd been able to "cure" him, I don't think I'd ever have been able to look at him the same way again.

So that's what I do now. I hunt down those things, and I take care of them.

Those things eat us, or worse, turn us into more of them.

That's not anything I'm gonna take sitting down.

One of the first things you asked me was, why was I talking about all this? Wasn't what we were doing meant to be a *secret*? Wouldn't my account possibly make the Indian authorities finally get to the bottom of all those mutilated corpses and wouldn't that threaten to implicate members of our organization?

I'll say here again, what I told you back then:

If the IPS *[the Bhāratīya Pulis Sevā, the Indian Police Service-Eds.]* get around to digging and if they're any good at their jobs, then they might just see the *anomalies*, the discrepancies. And if they do, maybe then the authorities in other parts of the world will wake up to the facts.

The organization I'm a part of, we're not really a secret society or anything like that. At least, we're not a secret to *them*.

The *aswang* have known about us for a *long* time, so this is just me—just *us*—reminding them that we're still out here, hunting down the monsters.

We are Legion, like the Good Book says.

We're *your* demons, you bastards.

We know about you, and now, the rest of the world is starting to know about you, too.

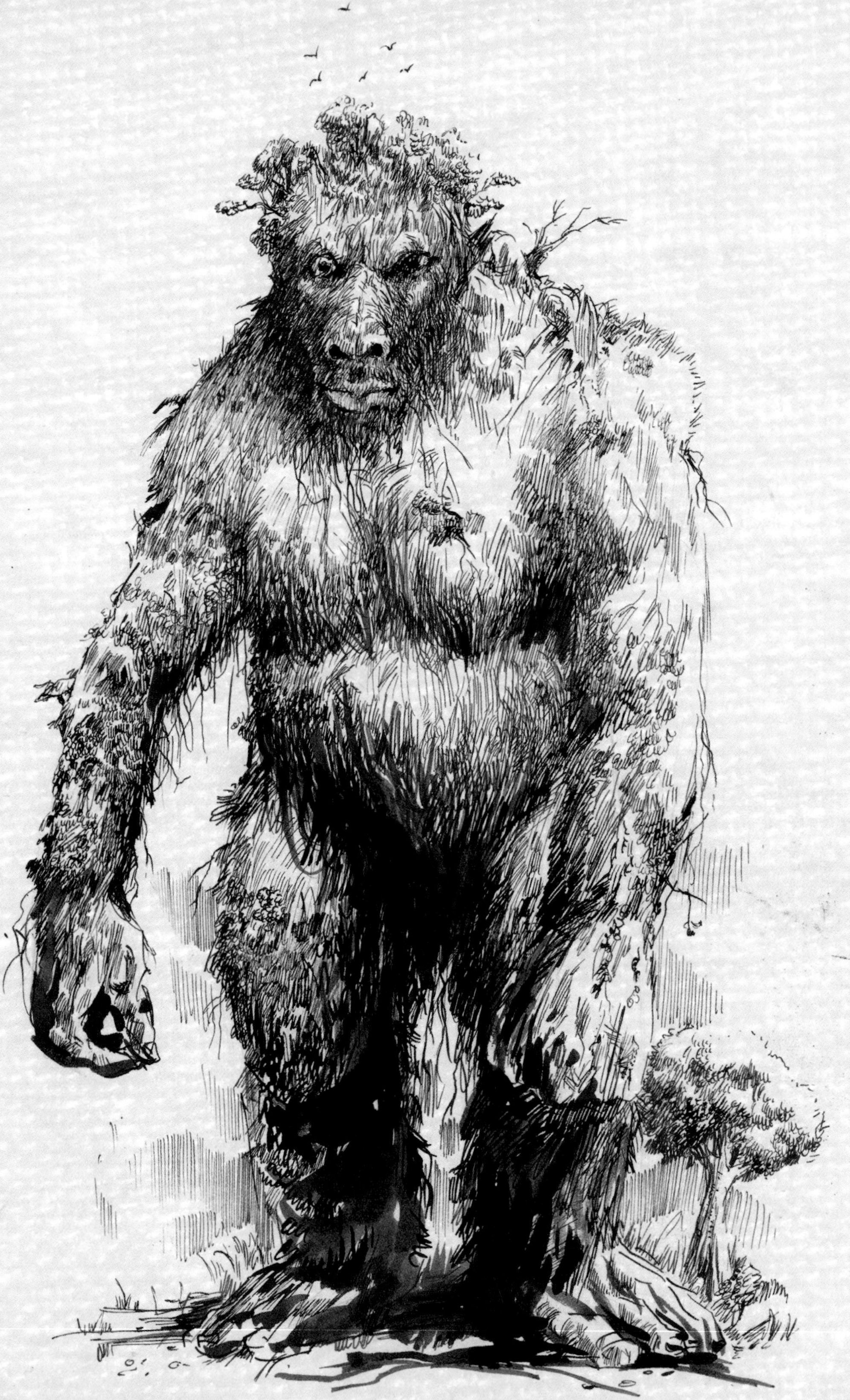

ANI-ANI

During the nights of the new moon, when the air is suddenly filled with the stench of a herd of a hundred goats, there is a possibility that an *Ani-ani* is in the vicinity. These cigar-smoking giants have sometimes been mistaken for mountains because of their size.

A sleeping *Ani-ani* was once found in the middle of the Pamulaklakin Forest in 1613. The villagers had plans to capture it and bring it back to their barrio, but when they returned the next day, the giant was gone and in its place was a towering cluster of talisay trees.

Witnesses say, during those moonless nights, they would encounter a hairy carabao, horse, or pig blocking the road, which would prevent them from venturing forward. When they try to scare away the animal, it would transform into the towering behemoth and chase them away by threatening to step on them.

One could only speculate on what the *Ani-ani* might be protecting.

We have spent one too many nights traveling up and down the roads of Zambales hoping to encounter this magical carabao, horse, swine. When we were confronted by a boar, we steeled ourselves and engaged with the animal—only to find out that it was an ordinary boar... which still made for a hearty meal.

On what must have been our 99th night of seeking out the Ani-ani, I yelled at the new moon and said I'd give my grandmother's golden locket if I could just meet an Ani-ani at that moment.

The horse I was on, my trusty steed for months, suddenly bucked and leapt and threw me off. It shed its equine form and became an ebony giant. It smiled, and its white teeth made it seem like the crescent moon suddenly appeared before me. I had no choice but to surrender my beloved locket, but in return I learned of another secret, which allowed me to discover an even greater treasure.

A. Pardo

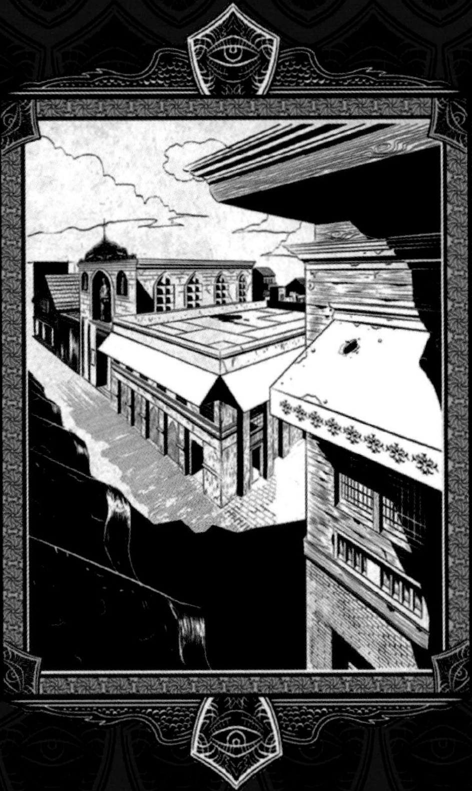

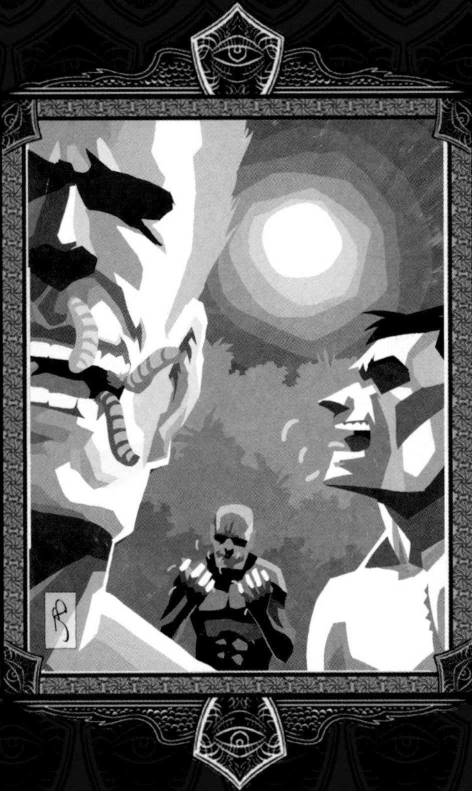

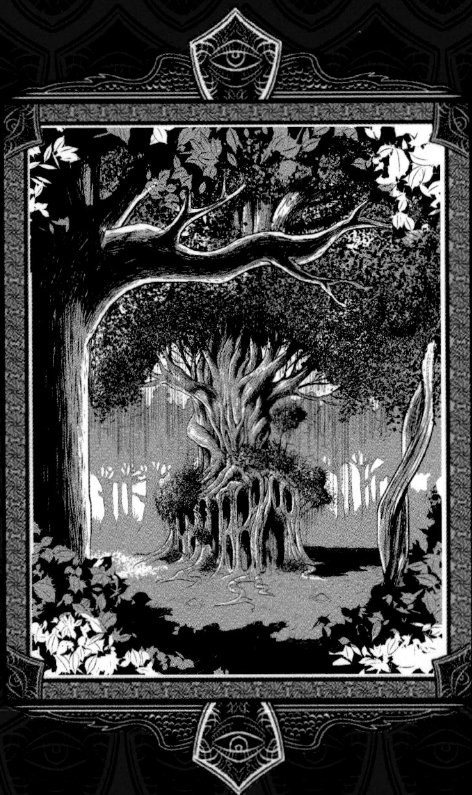

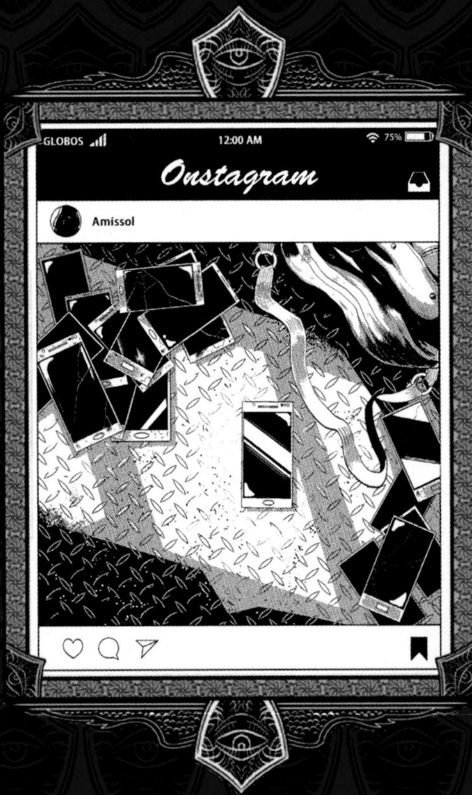
GLOBOS
12:00 AM
75%
Onstagram
Amissol

GUS
WHAT HAPPENS IN LOS SIMA

Since the witness of the following account did not elaborate on this crucial element of his story, I'll cover it in broad strokes here before we get to the account proper.

Los Sima.

For anyone who's even remotely interested in Filipino occult esoterica, Los Sima should be familiar. (Even for the more casual individual who normally cares nothing for the strange and unexplained, Los Sima became a household name for a few brief weeks in early November of last year, approximately half a year before the LJ was released.)

However, for the uninitiated...

Los Sima is a small town situated at the foot of Mount San Cristobal in Quezon. It was established by the Spaniards in the late 16th century, at a time when Luzon was known as Nueva Castilla.

Los Sima is notable for being a ghost town when invading Japanese forces came across it in the early months of 1942. Military records show that when Japanese soldiers first set foot in Los Sima, they discovered it completely deserted, without any evidence of what had befallen its population.

While there have been theories that have suggested that the Japanese simply made that claim to cover up the fact that they had slaughtered all the town's inhabitants, it should be noted that these same records indicate that while there were preliminary discussions about turning Los Sima into some kind of military outpost, a platoon spent a single night in the town, then left the morning after.

The Japanese never returned to Los Sima, and it was never converted into a military outpost. It has also remained uninhabited to this day.

In a curious footnote, in 1976, Hirai Makoto, a World War II veteran listed as having been part of that platoon that spent a single night in Los Sima, claimed that he and his compatriots experienced phenomena that convinced them the town was "norowareta," or "cursed."

He claimed that they heard noises coming from the nearby forest, unearthly music, laughter, and the sounds of construction—the hammering of nails, the sawing of wood—as if a large structure were being built in the heart of the forest.

Hirai also claimed that the following morning, a dozen men were missing, though military records list those men as having been Killed in Action.

Hirai also verified the fact that though there were intentions of turning Los Sima into an outpost, the events of that night dissuaded his superiors from that course of action.

The following account by Gus* is the first time his experience has been made public.

Before he sat down and recorded this session, he had only recounted his full experience in Los Sima to the investigating officers of the Philippine National Police, his management team, and select members of his family, as well as in the written document that he initially sent to our publisher.

My name's Angus, but everybody knows me as "Gus."

That's what's on all the billboards and magazine covers: Gus.

I had it good, you know? Before all that Los Sima shit. I was about to star in a fantaserye, man!

Shit.

Right.

Los Sima.

So we were 18, all in all, 13 models, me included, Kepano, the photographer, and a really small crew for the lights, make up, wardrobe—all for a guerrilla fashion shoot to buff up Kepano's online portfolio.

The fashion shoot had this horror theme, you know, so the location was Los Sima, and we shot on October 31. Kepano worked it all out so we'd wrap the shoot up late evening, and we'd all be free by midnight, so we could celebrate Halloween in this creepy abandoned ghost town.

And it was. Super fucking creepy.

We shot a bunch of stuff indoors, in those houses that looked like they'd been ripped right out of *Noli or El Fili*, that sort of look, you know.

And inside… Inside them, there was this weird kind of light, like no matter how bright and sunny it was outside, the light could never really get through the windows and into the houses? They were fucking gloomy.

But Kepano loved that light. He had a word for it… Creepustular? Something like that.

I just thought it was creepy as fuck.

So we wrapped about 9-ish, ate, plugged in our power banks, and turned the mobile data back on our phones… you know, for all our friends and followers and stans and stalkers.

We did all that social media shit then, 'cause we all knew the stuff that would come later was strictly for us. Like what happens in Los Sima, *stays* in Los Sima, you know?

And when we got all that stuff out of the way, Kepano gathered up all our phones and stashed them in the bus, and we were ready to party our brains out.

My *Lola*—my Mom's Mom—always said I had the "third eye." That I was "sensitive" or whatever. But that the eye was still "asleep," that it needed to be "opened" before I'd see that she was right.

Before Mom married Dad and moved to Canada, taking *Lola* with her, *Lola* was some kind of big deal *Manggagamot*, I think is the word? Like a magic woman healer? Something like that.

Dad always made fun of her, but never in front of her face.

I think my Dad was *scared* of Lola.

And I think she might have been right about my third fucking eye.

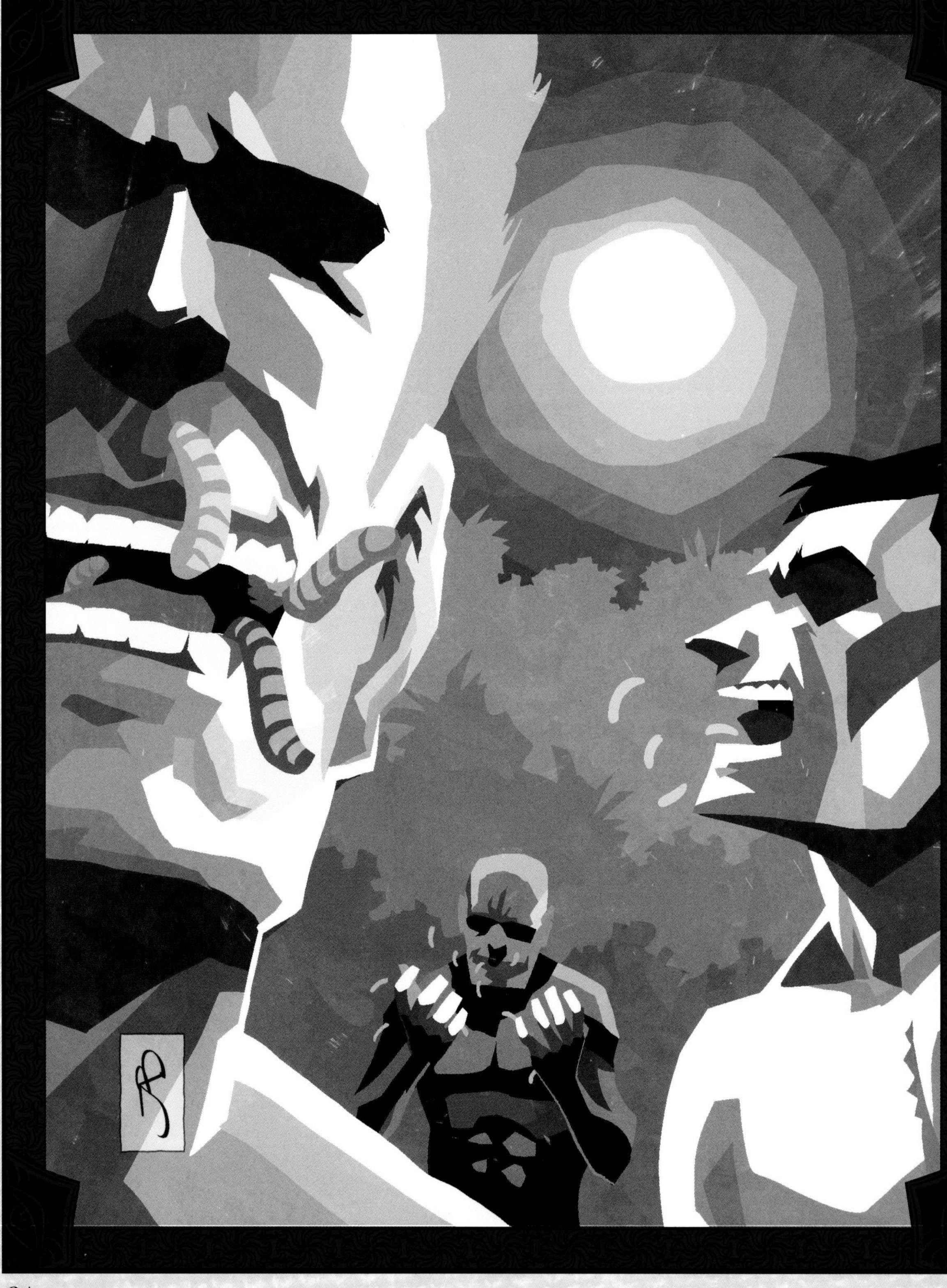

I really should have noticed it while it was happening, but I was too busy pitching Kepano on my photo shoot idea. (Plus, well, I was zonked out of my mind.)

I should have noticed that as we were closing in on midnight, people were acting just like in a *Friday the 13th*, or maybe a *Halloween*, since… you know… it was October 31.

People were hooking up and going off to wherever to get drunk, or high, or laid, or all three.

We were *splitting up*.

But like I said, I was busy trying to convince Kepano that we should have a kind of kickass Tony Jaa Muay Thai theme for our next shoot, maybe with elephants and stuff. Or some crazy parkour shit. A shoot where I could actually use some of the skills I've got, skills I was superserious about before I decided to try out this modeling career thing, skills I was ready to fucking unleash in the *fantaserye*.

But really, I was just ready to do any kind of shoot other than the Wes Carpenter shit we were doing in that creepyass town.

And then the screaming started.

The thing is though, *I* was the only one who could hear the screaming. Kepano and everyone else who was still with us at the town plaza where we'd built a bonfire, they heard laughter, like all the others who weren't with us were having the best time ever.

So it was like I was the only one in the horror movie. Everyone else was still enjoying some random *24 Hour Party People* scene.

The screams were coming from the forest, but I checked some of the houses I ran past, houses that I was sure some of the others had snuck into to do their own thing, throwing doors open, and shouting for them to come out. But those houses were *empty*.

I already knew it, even before I got there: Anyone who wasn't at the town plaza (and those guys were all following me since it looked like I was having a meltdown freakout), they were in the forest.

I thought they were the ones who were screaming, but when I found them, they were in a clearing, naked, and most of them were eating *worms*. They were just shoving those disgustoid worms into their mouths, and there was all this *screaming*, and this horrible stink.

And the humongous balete tree…which was actually a house…or maybe the *hole* that a house makes in the world…

Everyone I've told this story to thinks it was all just the alcohol and the drugs, and yeah, I was fucking loaded, but here's the thing: I think whatever it was I took that night opened my third eye, so I was seeing and hearing things everyone else who was there couldn't.

They all looked so *happy* while they were eating those worms.

And Kepano and the others who'd followed me into the forest…they acted like whatever it was they were seeing was the most *beautiful* thing they'd ever seen. Some of the others started eating the worms, too, and Kepano started to cry. He was like someone who'd been praying all his life, who'd finally gotten to see what God looked like. He was just looking at that tree or house, or hole, whatever it was, and he fell to his knees and cried.

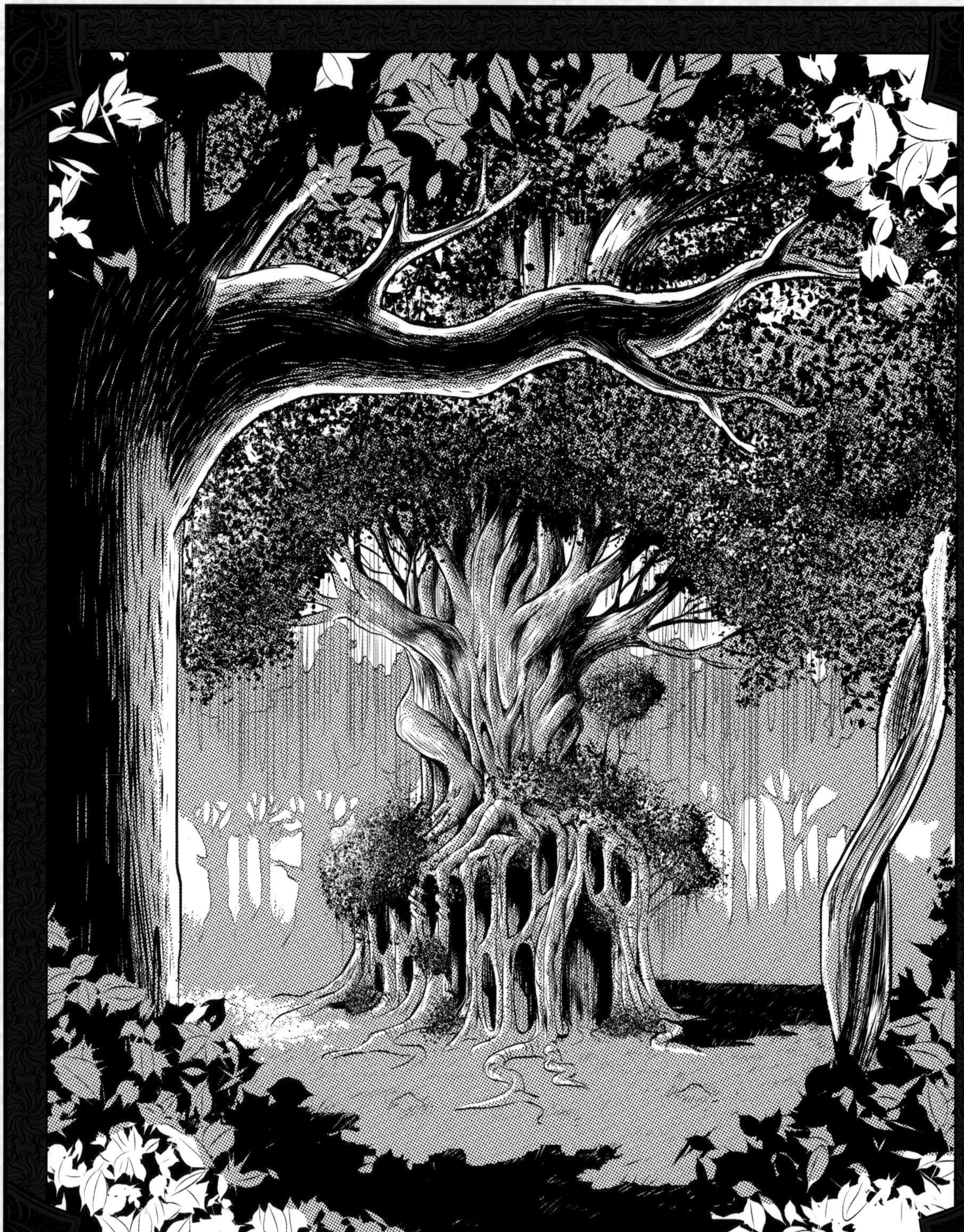

I don't know what he was seeing, but I was looking at the same thing he was, and looking at it just made me shit scared.

So I ran.

I ran and I ran and I ran…

I just ran until I found a road, and then I ran some more.

Finally, I saw some headlights and I waved at whoever it was to stop.

It was only when I heard the car stop, and the front door open, that I finally realized I was safe, and that's when I passed out.

It was all over the news, and I'm sure you saw the whole train wreck as it was happening.

17 people missing, no evidence at all at the scene that we were ever in Los Sima. No footprints, fingerprints, DNA shit, no litter, no sign of the bonfire, nothing. Not even the fucking bus!

The place looked like we never even got there.

But *all* the social media posts proved we'd been there, which confused all the cops and reporters even more.

I told my story to the "authorities," *[making exaggerated air quotes with his fingers]* but because I was obviously drunk and high and raving like a fucking lunatic when I woke up at the local clinic I was brought to, no one believed me.

And there was *actually* one hot moment when the cops looked at me like *maybe* I was a *suspect*, the fucking criminal mastermind who'd made 17 people and a fucking bus disappear into fucking thin air!

And right before they dropped the whole suspect idea anyway, some random (and sleazy- looking) cop guy made some very unsubtle suggestions that maybe I needed to pay up, because even though there wasn't any evidence now, didn't mean they might not suddenly find something tomorrow. He basically said, as long as I paid up, they'd conveniently forget that line of inquiry and they wouldn't suddenly "find" any new "evidence."

Assholes! Fucking stupid corrupt assholes!

But no bodies, no evidence, no foul play.

The only court I got judged in was the court of public opinion, and Los Sima *killed* me, strapped me down to the electric chair and then threw the fucking switch.

Rumors swirled on the Internet, what else is new, but some of them were so far from the truth, I would've laughed my a—s off if it wasn't me those rumors were about. And my management told me to keep my mouth shut, so I did.

Sure, the scandal was great for my social media profile, but there was just too much *mystery* there. People want simple, fast food solutions to their puzzles. They only want to be *pretend* challenged, like "What Color Is This Dress?" bullshit, and what happened to us at Los Sima was some aggressive and in-your-face weird shit, the kind most people pretend doesn't exist 'cause they can't break it down into numbers or ratings or a grade, they can't shove it into a little box and label it *'cause they don't know what it is, and worse, they don't know what it fucking means.*

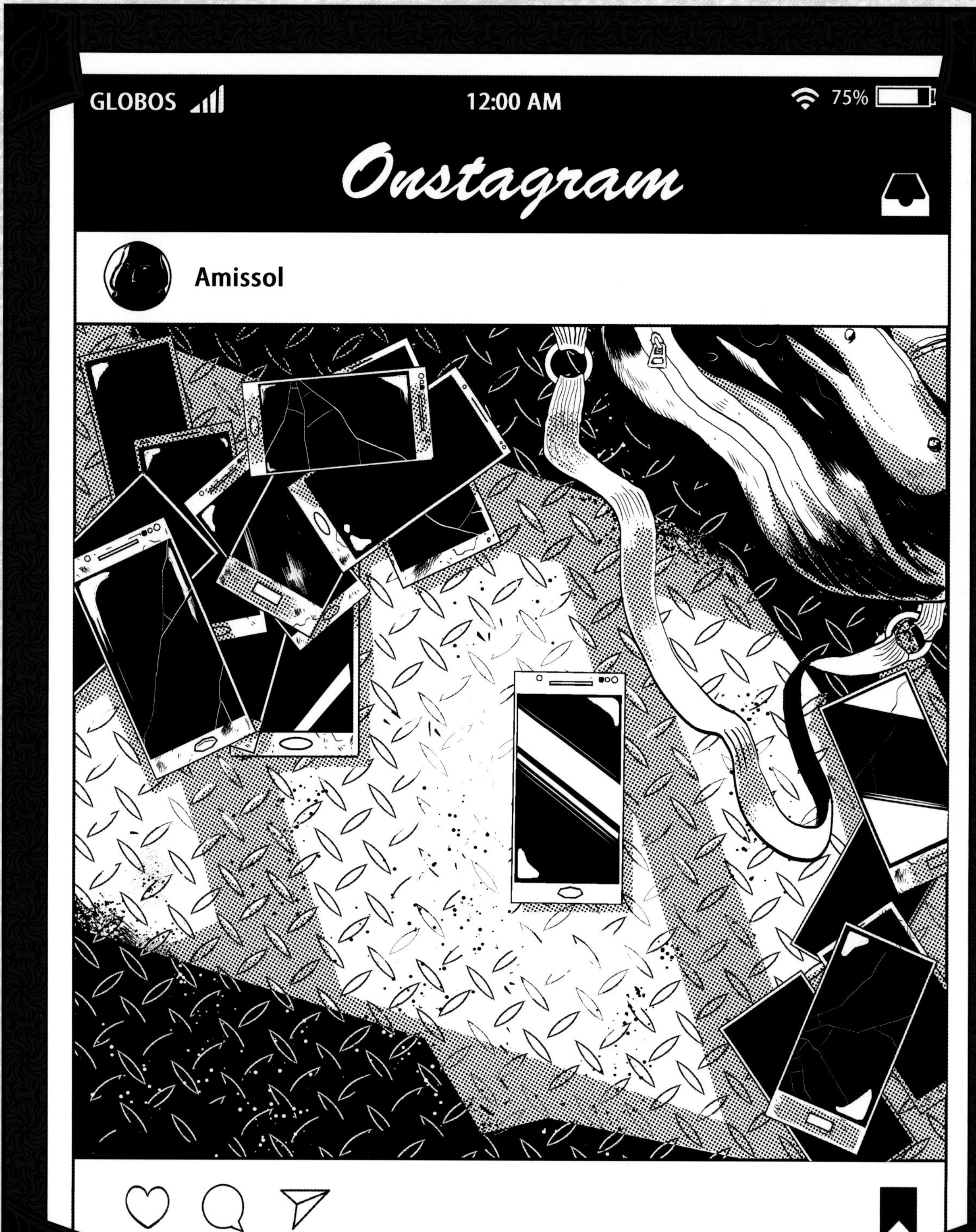
GLOBOS
12:00 AM
75%
Onstagram
Amissol

Plus, they lost a dozen of the most beautiful and handsome people on social media one dark and creepy Halloween for no obvious reason, and that's something the Internet just *cannot* forgive.

(At least for the few weeks or months before some *other* thing goes viral and gets memed and becomes the new thing people can get super-worked up about.)

In the end, I just got so sick of keeping my mouth shut, and after I saw *The Lost Journal*, I told my management team, "There. These guys get it. These guys know. I'm reaching out to them."

They weren't happy, but hell, I'm paying them, so I sent that letter, and you got in touch with me, and here I am, talking into this recorder.

There's one more thing about that night in Los Sima, something no one's ever mentioned, something no one's ever noticed, except me. (Or maybe, someone *did* notice, but decided not to bring it up anymore, 'cause it only raised more questions.)

There was one last post on Kepano's feed that went up at exactly midnight, and if my sense of time wasn't completely fucked up by the shit I was on, midnight was way after I saw Kepano last, on his knees and crying his eyes out at whatever it was he was seeing.

That last post was a picture of all of our cellphones, on the floor of the bus. They were in three groups: the biggest was a dozen, the phones of all the other models; then there was a single phone, mine; and then, the last five, the phones of the crew and Kepano.

I believe that post was meant for me, and I think I know what it means.

Whatever lives in that house…it took the other models. In my whacked-out memories of that clearing, it was only the other models who were eating those worms, none of the crew touched those worms, and I never saw Kepano eat them either.

The crew's and Kepano's phones were separated 'cause they weren't taken. Whatever lives in that house didn't want them. I don't know where they are, or what happened to them, but I hope they're dead, because even back then, I already felt like entering that house would be the worst thing that could ever happen to anyone.

And my phone, alone.

Because I got away.

And because I think whatever lives in that house still wants me.

Every time I see myself in the mirror, I'm reminded of why it might still want me…

Oh, and one other thing.

If that post showed all of our phones, then whose phone was used to take the pic?

---

* As is the case with my identity, anyone who hasn't been living in a cave or a deserted island without WiFi will know that "Gus" is a pseudonym, but again, as per our publisher's wishes, he is Gus within these pages.

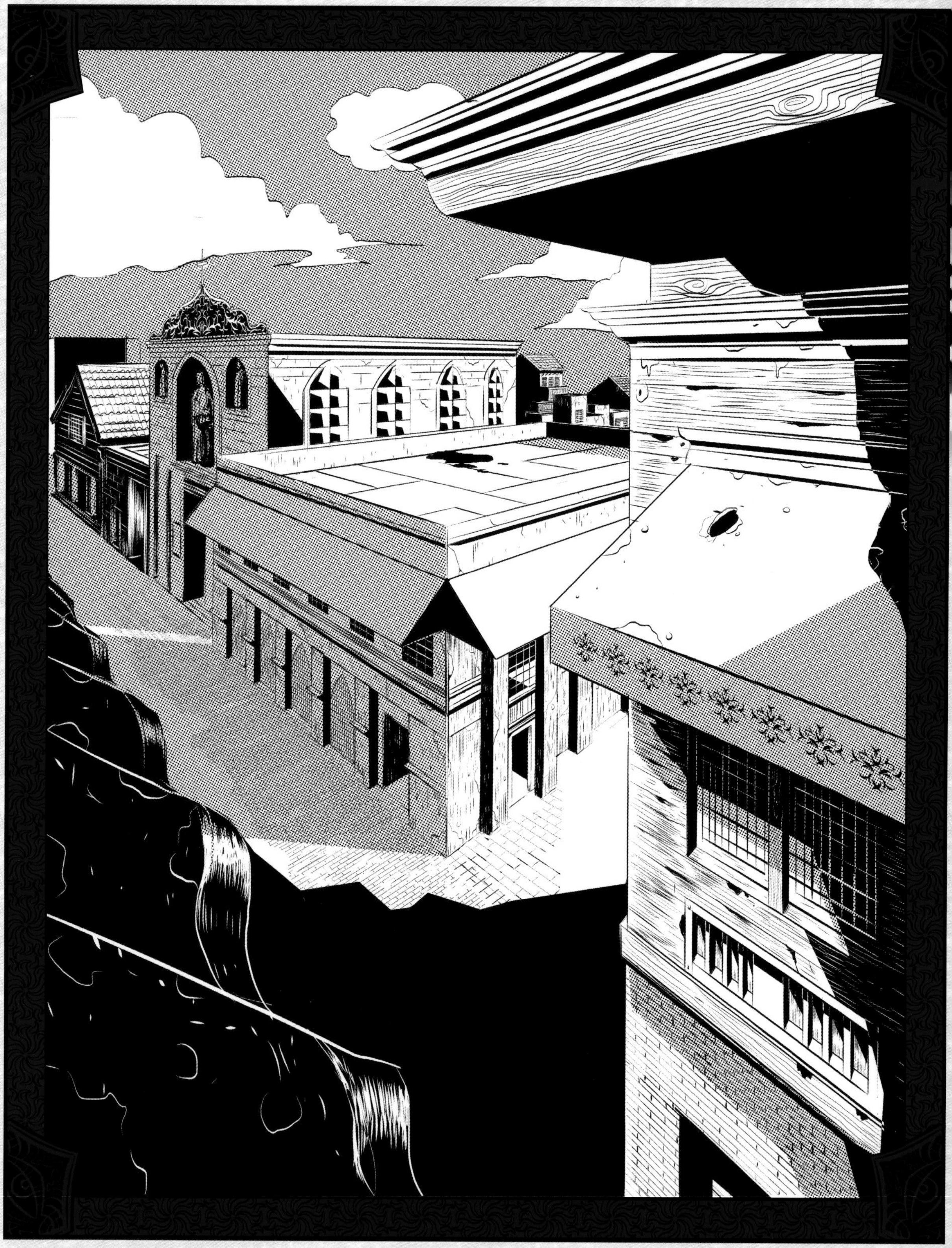

Now I'd like to note a number of things.

ONE:
Some balete trees are strangler figs, or, in more scientific terms, hemiepiphytes. These are plants that grow around a host tree, "strangling" it.

This process usually results in the death of the host (or support) tree, and the strangler fig then becomes a "columnar" tree, with a hollow core where the host tree once was.

TWO:
In my research of Spanish folklore, I came across some brief references to something called *La Casa Hueca* ("The Hollow House"). This was said to be, alternately, a house inside a tree, a tree in the shape of a house, or a tree that encompassed the "absence of a house" (whatever that may mean).

The Spanish word used to describe what *La Casa Hueca* was capable of doing to those who even so much as looked upon it, is "arrebatar," which means, among other things, "snatch,, "carry away," or "enrapture."

THREE:
Records show that among those living in Los Sima in 1941 (and thus, presumably also among those missing when the Japanese arrived in the deserted town) was noted architect Jose N. Antonio.

Antonio was born in Los Sima, but studied in Spain and thereafter made a name for himself in his field, before returning to his hometown upon his retirement.

Antonio's architectural work was known for its "unearthly and elegant beauty" and "rapturous magnificence."

FOUR:
About a week after I sat down with Gus to record his account, he took a straight razor to his face.

Though the wounds were severe, they were also purely cosmetic.

It was not a suicide attempt.

Gus parted ways with his management team and is now a permanent resident of the same compound I'm living in.

He is also currently under the psychological care of Dr. Emily Claire (an interview with her can be found in the section entitled *Dealing With the Dark*).

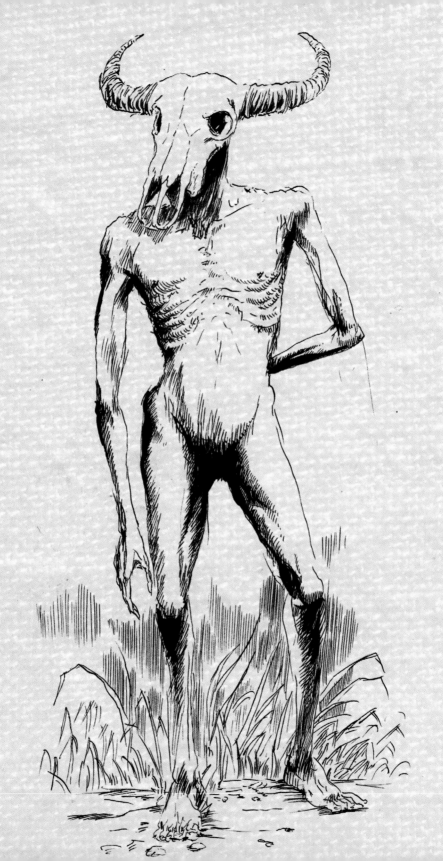

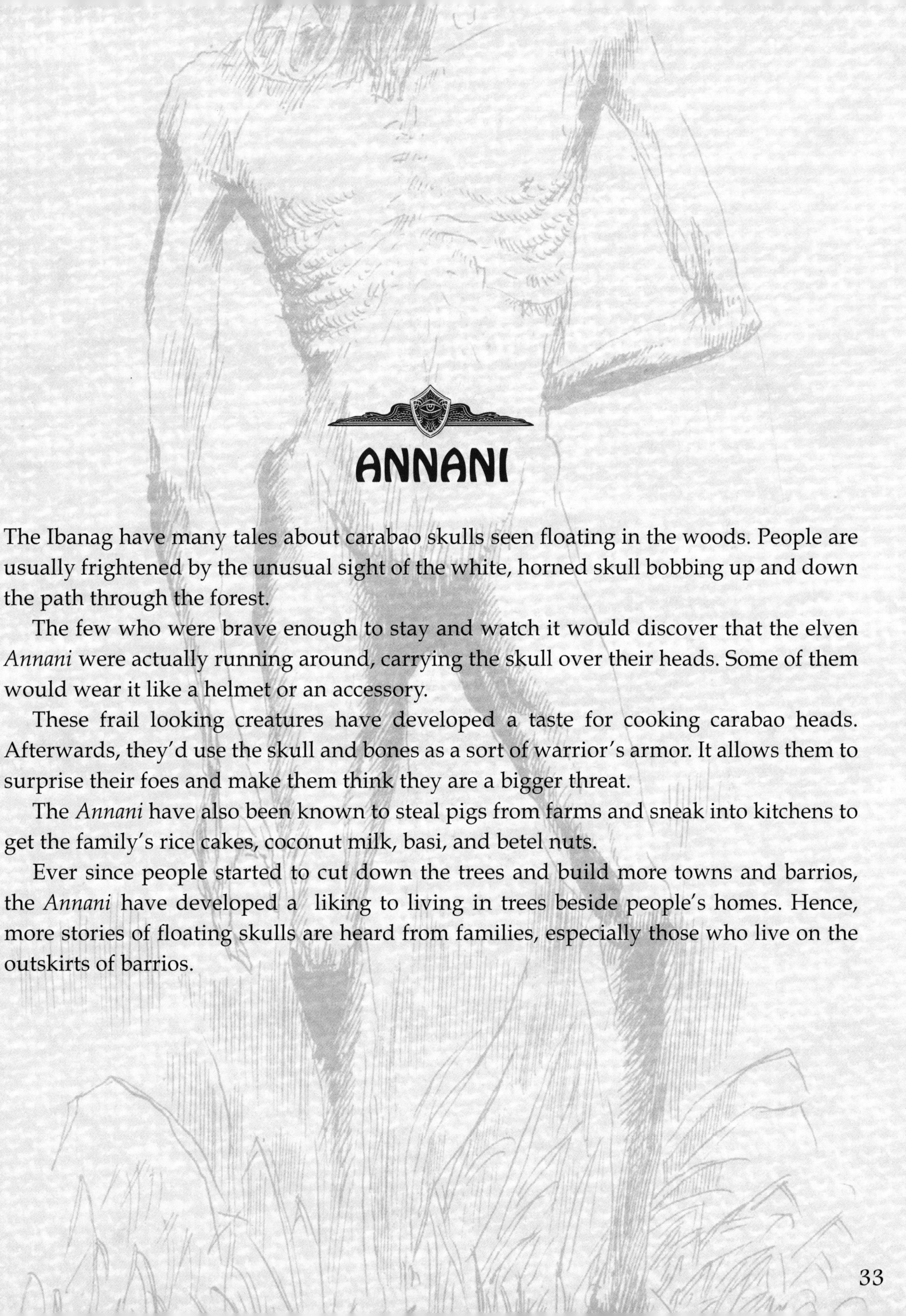

ANNANI

The Ibanag have many tales about carabao skulls seen floating in the woods. People are usually frightened by the unusual sight of the white, horned skull bobbing up and down the path through the forest.

The few who were brave enough to stay and watch it would discover that the elven *Annani* were actually running around, carrying the skull over their heads. Some of them would wear it like a helmet or an accessory.

These frail looking creatures have developed a taste for cooking carabao heads. Afterwards, they'd use the skull and bones as a sort of warrior's armor. It allows them to surprise their foes and make them think they are a bigger threat.

The *Annani* have also been known to steal pigs from farms and sneak into kitchens to get the family's rice cakes, coconut milk, basi, and betel nuts.

Ever since people started to cut down the trees and build more towns and barrios, the *Annani* have developed a liking to living in trees beside people's homes. Hence, more stories of floating skulls are heard from families, especially those who live on the outskirts of barrios.

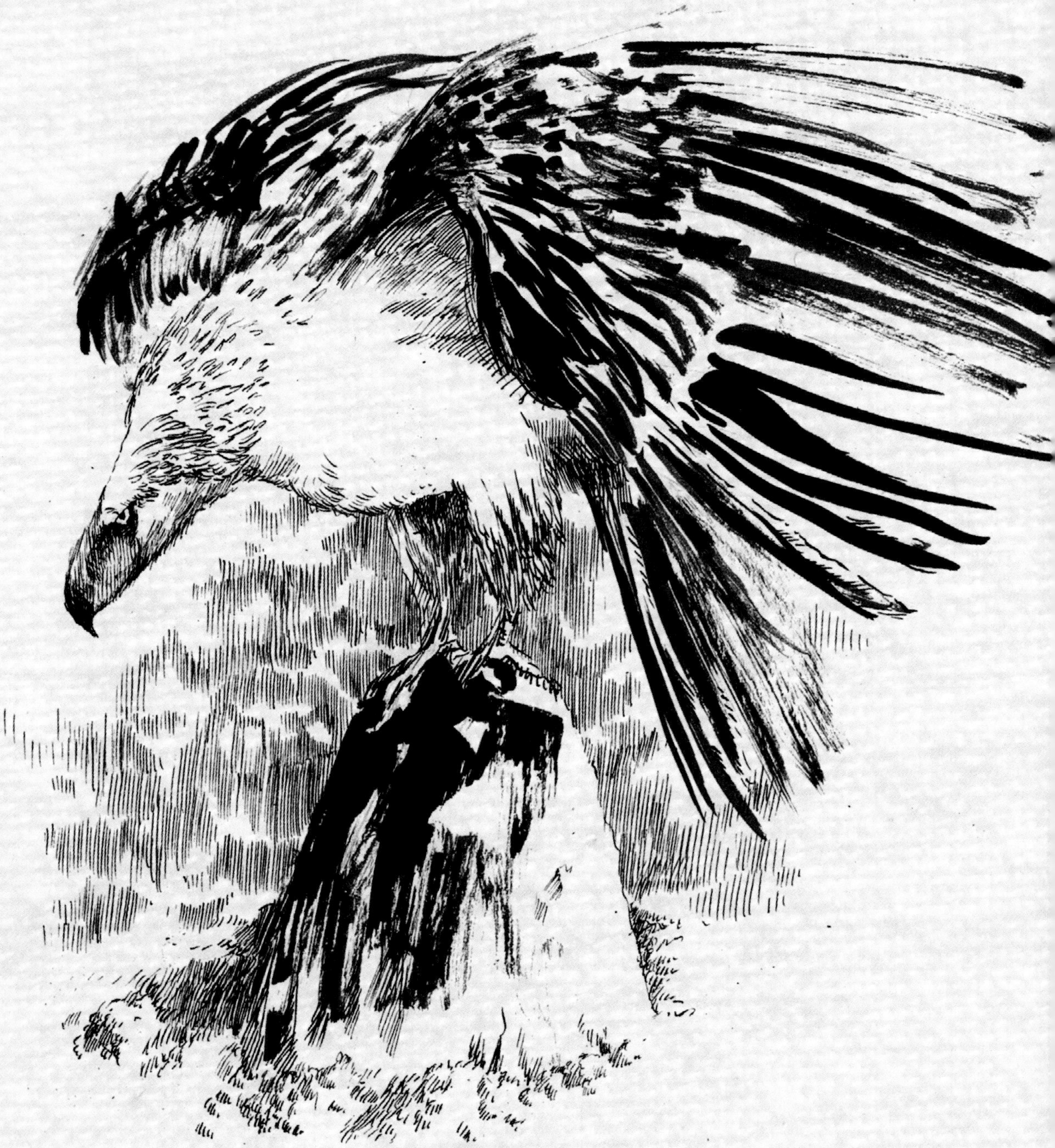

BAWA

After a typhoon, just as the storm clouds begin to part and a moment before the sun pierces through the grey, look towards the horizon and you might just see a hole in the sky. To the tribes of Western Visayas, this is the cave known as Calulundan, others call it the Baua Cave. Inside this cave, sleeps the gargantuan bird of prey known as the *Bawa*.

Every couple of years, the *Bawa* would grow hungry and venture out of its cave. Its thunderous screech would be heard for miles. The flapping of its wings would bring typhoon-strong winds to the villages on its flight path.

When it hungers, it would either attempt to eat the sun or the moon. The tribes of Hiligaynon believe that in that time before man, it was the gods who fought with the *Bawa* and prevented it from completely devouring our sun and moon. Later on, whenever an eclipse would happen, the tribes would bring out their weapons and create a lot of noise to scare off the *Bawa* and make it spit out its chosen celestial dish.

In one of our expeditions, we encountered a group of hunters armed with swords that were so light a baby could lift them, but the blades were sharp enough to cut through armor. They claim these came from the fallen feathers of the Bawa. We tried to buy the swords from the hunters with our gold, but they would not part with them. We now search for this cave called Calulundan and will dare to gather as much of these deadly feathers as we can.

A. Pardo

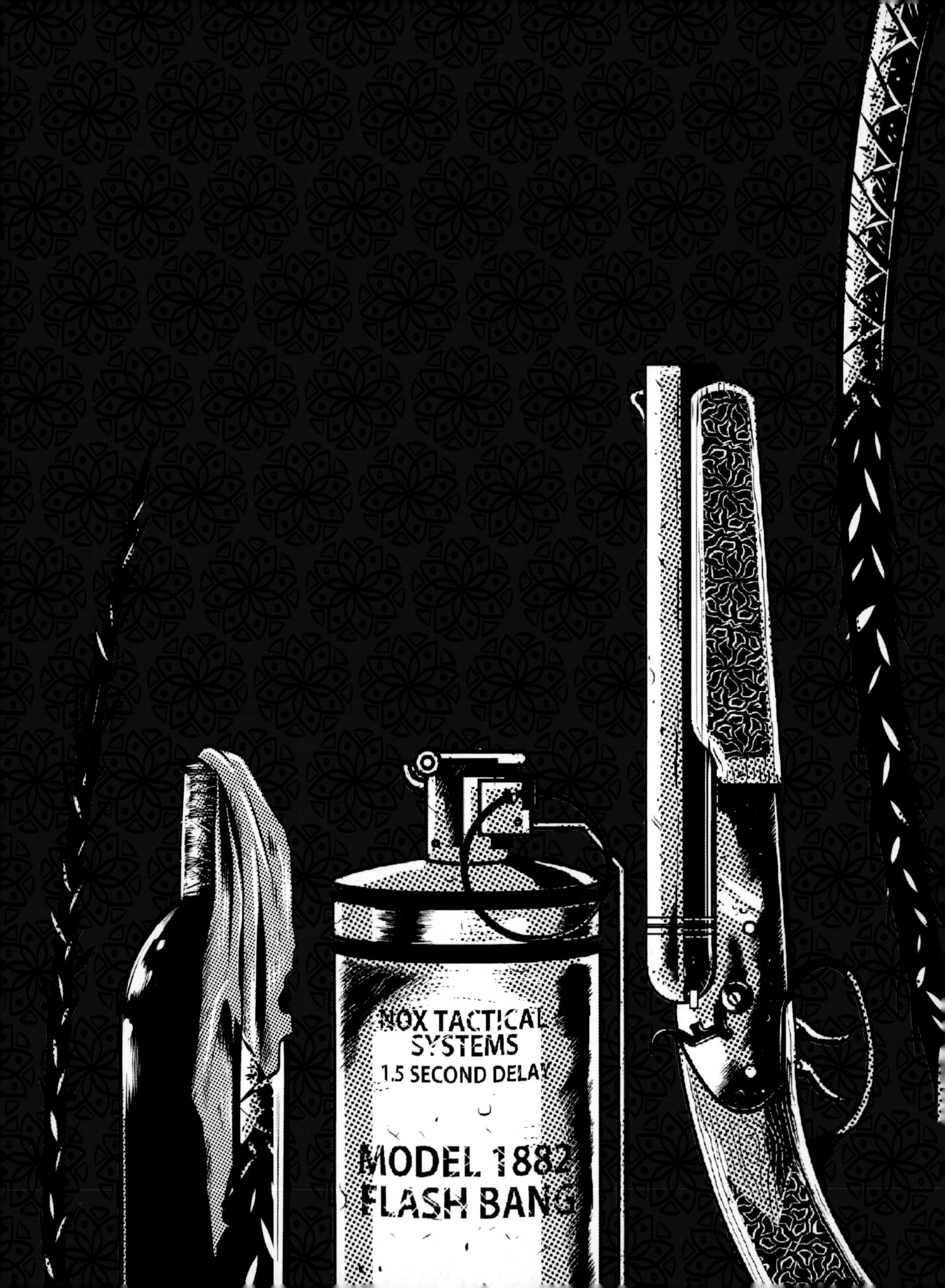
NOX TACTICAL
SYSTEMS
1.5 SECOND DELAY
MODEL 1882
FLASH BANG

DEFENDING AGAINST THE DARK: CONTEMPORARY WEAPONRY

I've never liked guns.

I managed to keep this mindset all throughout college, despite the fact that there were quite a number of military brats in my *barkada*. (Yes, these were geek military brats, all guns and paintball and RPGs, which is to say, not just rocket-propelled grenades, but also, role playing games.)*

No childhood trauma attached to that feeling—I've just never really liked them.

And seeing *Bowling for Columbine* just sealed the deal.

The way Hollywood fetishistically observes (in arty slow motion, no less) the tinkling rain of empty cartridges falling to the floor as the firearm expels bullet after bullet in an ejaculatory barrage does nothing but repulse me in the worst possible way.

It's safe to say guns and me just do not mix.

Seriously, this is a weapon that reduces a single human life to the cost of around 12 pesos (by today's exchange rate; who knows how much cheaper a life can get when the economy takes a downturn?).

This is a weapon that can be (and has been) discharged by *two-year-olds*.

I may not like knives much either, but for you to use one as a weapon takes *conviction*. It takes grabbing that handle and getting right up close, sharing the other person's body heat, maybe even looking them right in the face, and then feeling the jarring impact in your arm as the blade drives on home.

Conviction.

With a gun, the action is reduced to something impersonal and automatic, like flicking a light switch off from a distance.

With a gun, a life can be lost because of 12 pesos and a two-year-old.

When I first decided that, yes, I was going to move into the compound, this was one of my biggest worries: that I would find myself smack dab in the middle of an entire arsenal of guns and hosts of paranoid, twitchy trigger fingers.

To my gratified surprise, this is *far* from the case.

Not to say that there aren't any guns here. There are. (R.J.'s personal collection alone—which she stores in the compound—probably counts as an "arsenal" in and of itself.)

But many of the guns here don't fire regular ammunition.

Why would they, when it isn't really other humans we're concerned about?

The most common firearms I've seen are shotguns loaded with rock salt shells, which are highly effective against *aswang*.

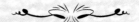

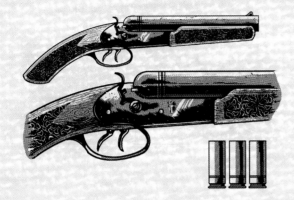

I've also seen shotguns loaded with gas shells, that contain a chemical agent that replicates smoke from burning garlic and carabao horn shavings, again effective against *aswang*. (I'm told that, among other things, the chemical agent is derived from keratin and allyl methyl sulfide.)

Others (like the members of the society R.J. is a part of) use buckshot filled with iron pellets, against *aswang*, *manananggal*, or *busaw*.

Flashbangs (stun grenades) are also popular. With their combination of a bright, blinding flash of light and the deafening sound (greater than 170 decibels), flashbangs are particularly effective deterrents against *ebwa*.

M 22
NOX TACTICAL
SYSTEMS
1.5 SECOND DELAY
MADE IN THE U.S.A.

Others prefer smoke bombs, which release the same kind of smoke as the gas shells mentioned earlier. (R.J. and her compatriots use smoke grenades, though these are more expensive than smoke bombs.)

Molotov cocktails are also both effective and cheap. Aside from merely gasoline, the liquid in the bottles also contains other ingredients, such as vinegar, garlic, onion, pepper, salt, and crushed ginger (for *kapre*), or lemon and kalamansi (again, for *aswang*).

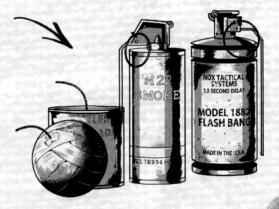

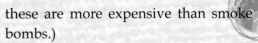

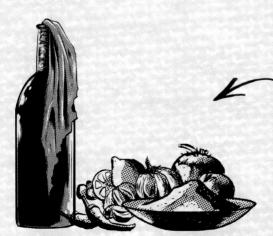

Aside from these customized modern weapons, I have also seen a number of *buntot pagi* (as described in the LJ) in the compound arsenal, as well as a number of other, more unique melee weapons. (See "Defending Against the Dark: *Cakar* and *Ekor*".)

Still, flashlights equipped with tanning bulbs (yes, as in those found in tanning beds) which emit UVA *[Ultraviolet A-Eds.]* light, are probably more my personal style.

With wavelengths from 315 to 400 nanometers, UVA is less dangerous than the shorter wavelength UVB or UVC to humans.

To creatures like the *manananggal*, however, UVA can be fatal. But even though I'd much rather pretend to be some *X-Files* Special Agent and use my moody and visually-arresting high-powered UVA flashlight to take down the next *manananggal* I see, I have to admit, I do have a gun.

Yes, even though I hate the ugly little things.

When I first moved in, I was given a choice to take temporary quarters at the very center of the compound dormitories.

I was told that this was offered to all newcomers. For a few moments after I was asked the question, I wondered why that was.

Then it hit me: this was the 21st century occult survivalist version of children wanting to sleep at the very *center* of the *banig*, away from the windows (and, let's face it, so there are a whole bunch of other warm bodies the nocturnal predator can get to before they arrive at little old you).

The idea was, if you needed help in acclimating to the new environment, feeling that extra bit of security at being nestled at the very center—at the very heart—of the compound couldn't hurt. And when you were more at ease and settled, and if there were any new arrivals to the compound, you would be moved to new quarters elsewhere in the dormitories.

Given my state when I first arrived, it was an offer I greatly appreciated, though ultimately, respectfully declined.

I chose other quarters in the dormitories, because I still wanted to be proactive enough that if I so chose, I could make my way to an exit, whereas being at the very center meant you were, in all likelihood, fully depending on everyone else standing up to and taking down whatever random creature chose to attack the compound.

I may not be anything like R.J., but sitting by and watching everyone else do something concrete and decisive was never my thing.

And like I said, should the time come and I need to use it, I have a gun.

See?

Even now I can't think of it as "my" gun.

Then again, in a way, it really isn't, even if it was given to me.

It's a .45 caliber M1911, and R.J. gave it to me shortly after I moved into the compound. But even though she gave it to me, I always think of it as something—a chafing dish, a coffee maker—that she lent to me, because she has so many others in her cupboards.

So I have a gun, but even though I do, I'm not under any illusions that I'm suddenly an expert at Gun Fu.

I know my limitations, and if any random creature does decide to attack the compound, and somehow gets through all those other, better trained individuals with their shotguns and flashbangs and Molotov cocktails and *buntot pagi*, then there's very little I could probably do to stop it.

Which is why there's only one bullet in the gun. (And here, I'm taking my cue from R.J. and her compatriots, who always carry a spare bullet somewhere on their person.)

Only one bullet, in the firing chamber; the magazine is there, but it's empty.

One bullet.

I don't want to use it, of course, but I'd rather that, than become prey to some kind of monster, or worse, *become* some kind of monster.

I hope it doesn't come to that.

Please don't let it come to that.

But if it does…

If it does, I'll try not to think this horrible, ludicrous thought: that in the end *everything* I ever did in my life—all those decades and years and months and hours and minutes and seconds—that *all of that life*, was all just worth less than the price of one mini cup of instant noodles.

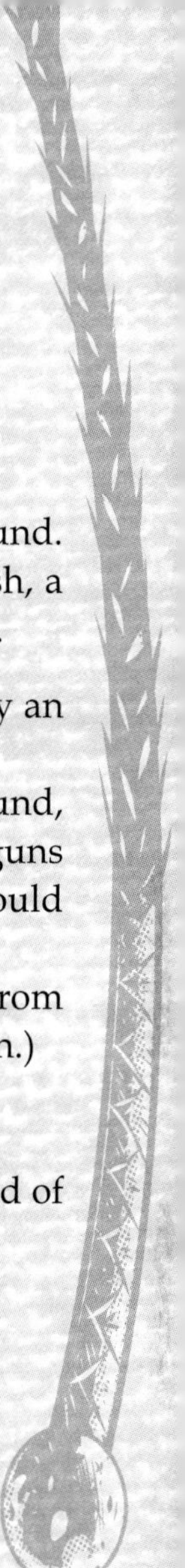

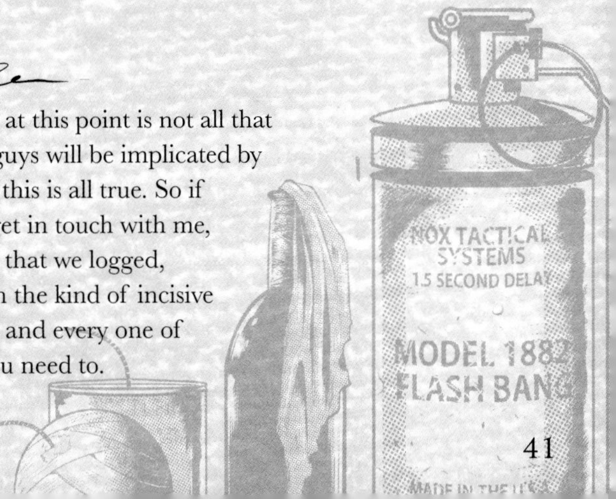

* As I mentioned in the Foreword, uncovering my identity at this point is not all that difficult. Given that, it's only a matter of time before you guys will be implicated by having known me. I'm so sorry for that. Trust me though, this is all true. So if ever you find yourselves in a situation where you need to get in touch with me, *be smart*, and *be careful*. And after all those hours of gaming that we logged, hours in which you planned and plotted and schemed with the kind of incisive precision only geek military brats could have, I know each and every one of you can be both. I know you'll be able to find me when you need to.

NOX TACTICAL
SYSTEMS
1.5 SECOND DELAY

MODEL 1882
FLASH BANG

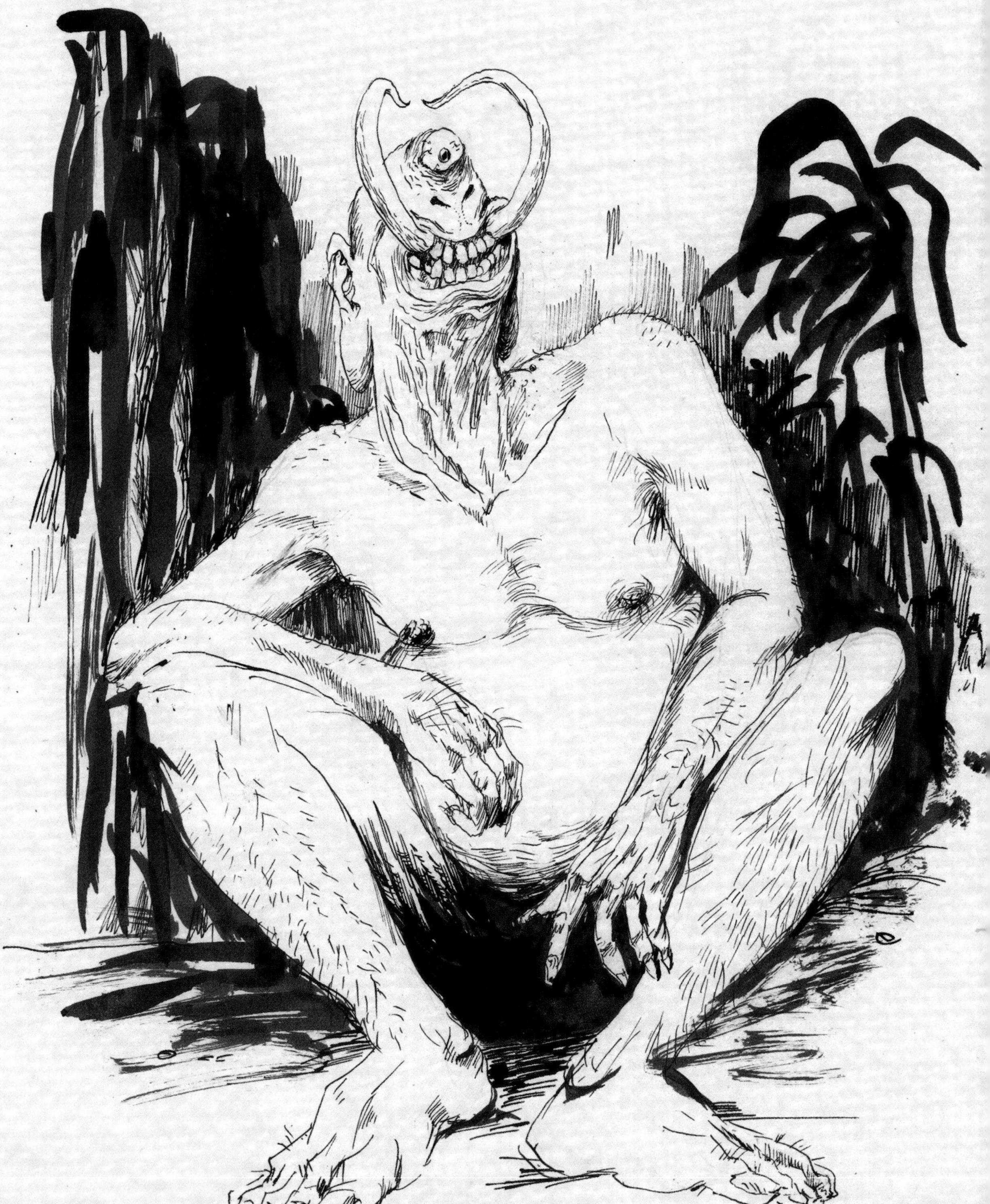

BUNGISNGIS

This cyclopean giant is a great hunter. Despite having only one eye, it does have a very uncanny hearing ability that allows it to distinguish the sounds made by its prey versus everything else in the vicinity.

Its name is derived from the word "*ngisi*," which means "to show one's teeth." The *Bungisngis* normally shows all its teeth if it is pleased or is ready to attack its enemy. It uses its two large tusks to lift and incapacitate its foe.

The laugh of the *Bungisngis* sounds like the chittering of insects trying to chew their way through wood. The more it's winning the battle, the louder it laughs.

A witness claims to have once seen a *Bungisngis* lift a carabao with just one hand. It then slammed the beast on the ground, creating a knee-deep crater in the earth.

We encountered this monstrosity on one of the mountain trails of Batangas. While it was a very formidable foe, it has, to our surprise, a very shallow sense of humor—which proved to be its downfall.

While attempting to defend myself with a large rock, I accidentally stumbled backwards, and the rock fell on the foot of my poor colleague. This little scene made the *Bungisngis* laugh at our expense. It laughed so hard, its huge upper lip was thrown back, and it completely covered its face. The hysterical giant fell down laughing, allowing us to defeat it.

A. Pardo

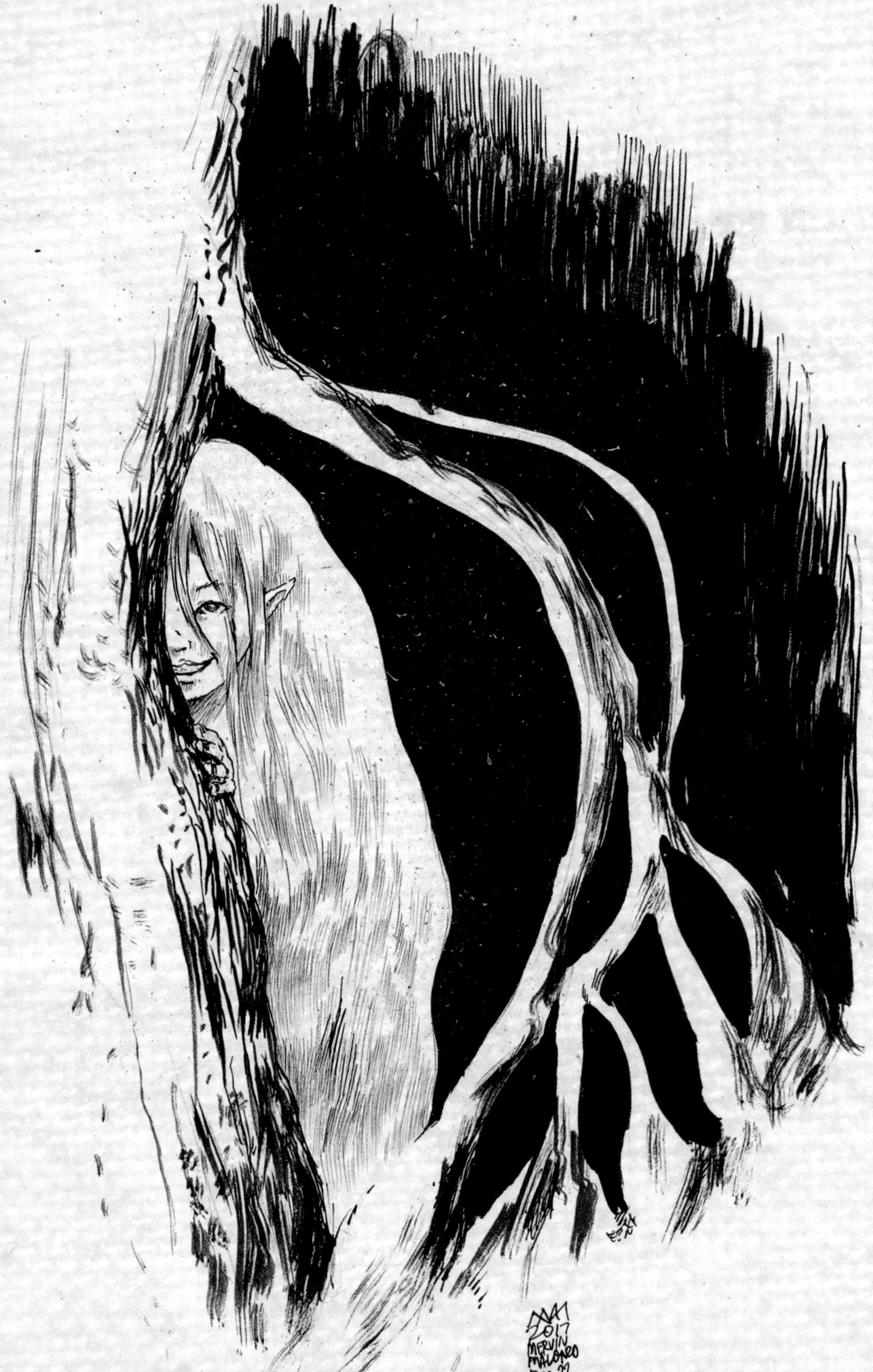
2017
MERVIN
MALONZO
Dec 22

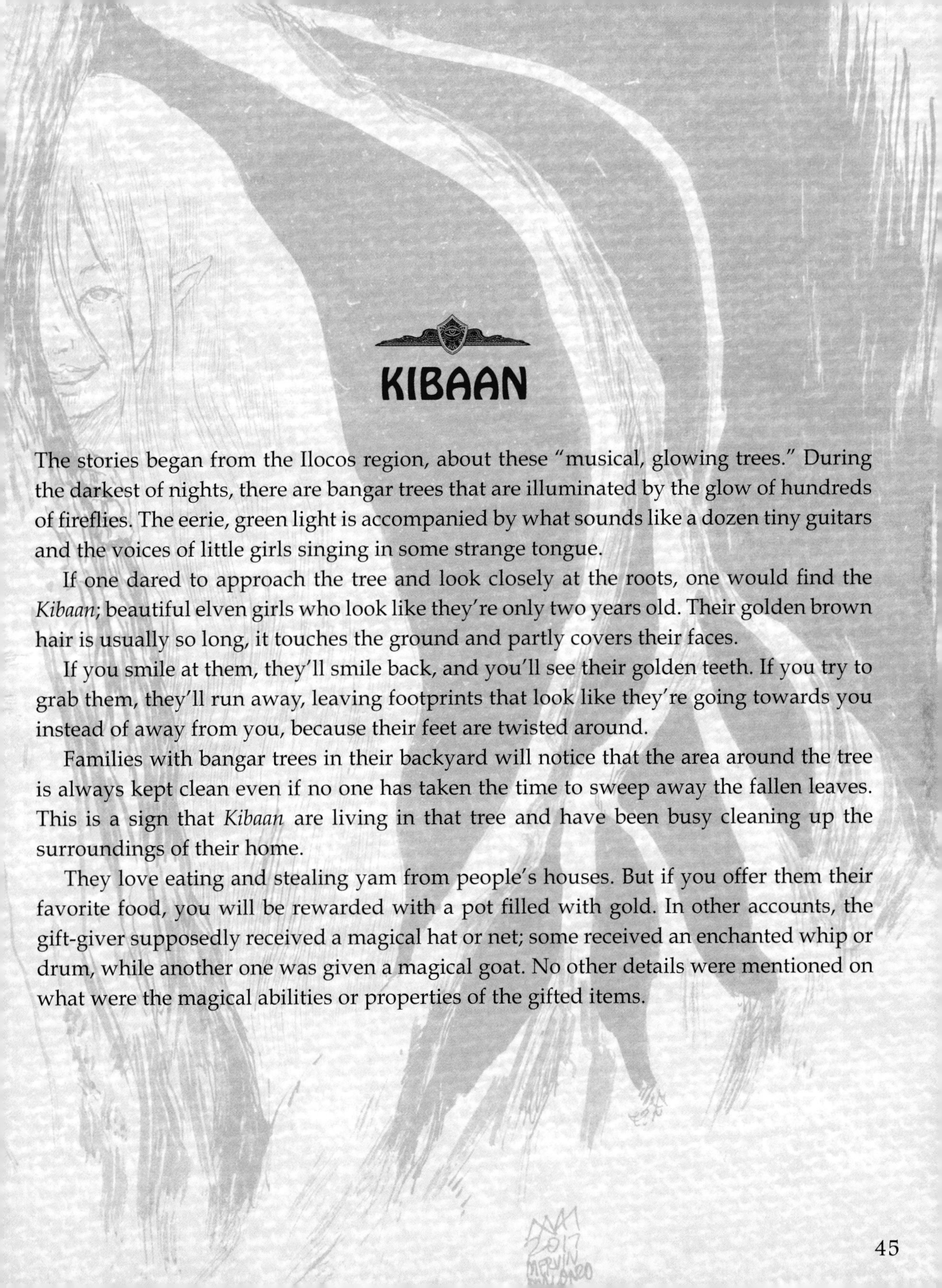

KIBAAN

The stories began from the Ilocos region, about these "musical, glowing trees." During the darkest of nights, there are bangar trees that are illuminated by the glow of hundreds of fireflies. The eerie, green light is accompanied by what sounds like a dozen tiny guitars and the voices of little girls singing in some strange tongue.

If one dared to approach the tree and look closely at the roots, one would find the *Kibaan*; beautiful elven girls who look like they're only two years old. Their golden brown hair is usually so long, it touches the ground and partly covers their faces.

If you smile at them, they'll smile back, and you'll see their golden teeth. If you try to grab them, they'll run away, leaving footprints that look like they're going towards you instead of away from you, because their feet are twisted around.

Families with bangar trees in their backyard will notice that the area around the tree is always kept clean even if no one has taken the time to sweep away the fallen leaves. This is a sign that *Kibaan* are living in that tree and have been busy cleaning up the surroundings of their home.

They love eating and stealing yam from people's houses. But if you offer them their favorite food, you will be rewarded with a pot filled with gold. In other accounts, the gift-giver supposedly received a magical hat or net; some received an enchanted whip or drum, while another one was given a magical goat. No other details were mentioned on what were the magical abilities or properties of the gifted items.

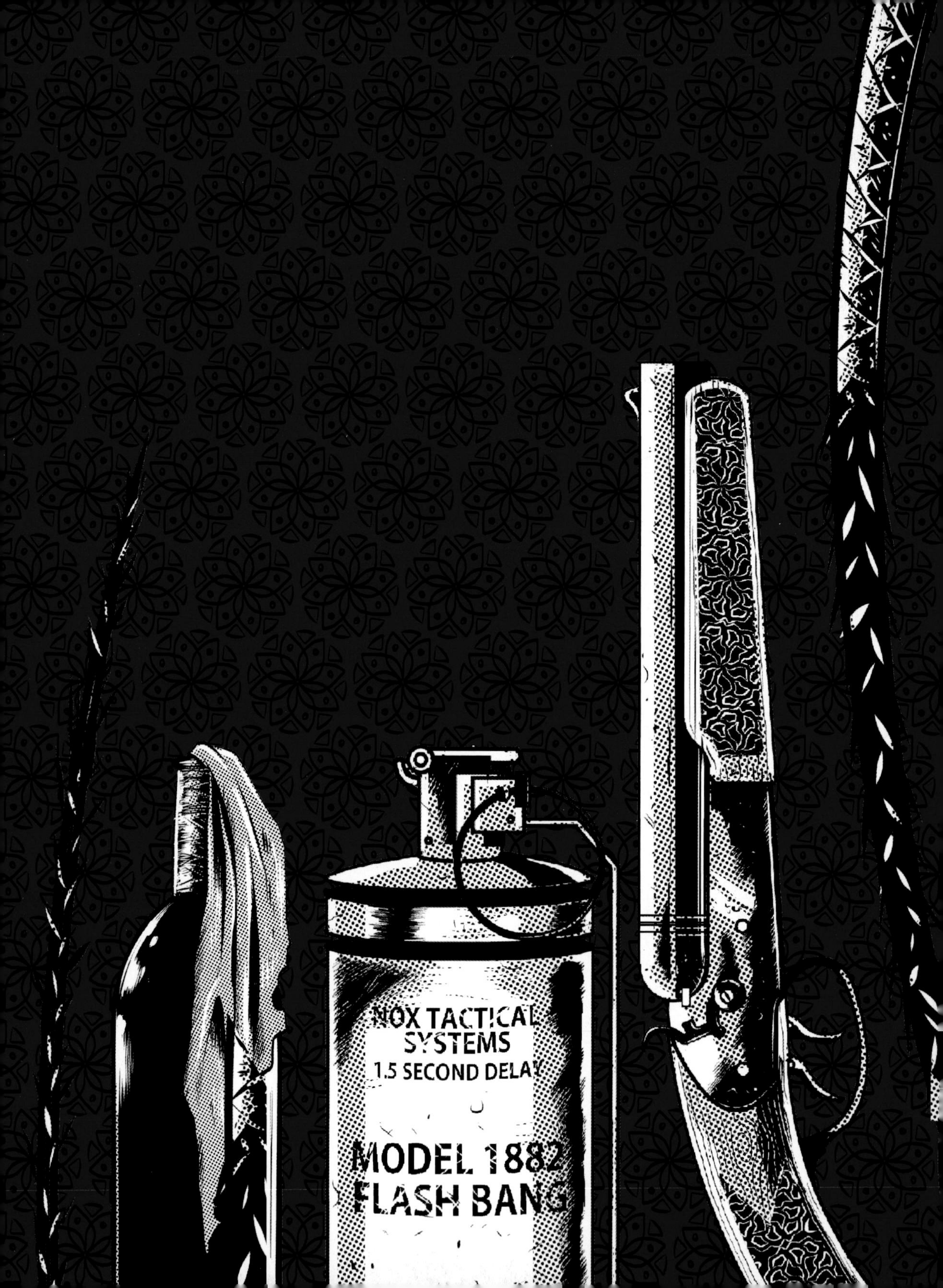
NOX TACTICAL
SYSTEMS
1.5 SECOND DELAY
MODEL 1882
FLASH BANG

DEALING WITH THE DARK

Ever since I became a resident of the compound, I've met several individuals who have become invaluable to all the hard work that has gone into the book you're currently holding in your hands. People like Alton Landau, Hermenegildo Romero (both of whom you will hear more about in a later section), and Dr. Emily Claire.

Emily (as she prefers to be called, even if you're a patient of hers) is a licensed clinical psychologist who specializes in cases involving what she refers to as "supranormal trauma."

We delve into what the term means in the Q&A below. The interview was conducted shortly after Gus became her patient.

Me: So how is Gus? Generally speaking, of course—patient confidentiality and all that.

EC: *He's actually doing quite well, considering what he's been through. He also told me to make sure you knew that I have his written consent, so we can go into details, so long as I feel, personally and as a professional, that any disclosure I make concerning his case won't hinder his recovery. He's freely admitted he needs to stop overindulging in drugs and alcohol, and he really does need a clear head if he wants to get a proper handle on all the…craziness his recently opened third eye will usher into his life.*

So, yes, he's doing well, but he really should have been sent to me as soon as the authorities released him. What he did was rather crude—almost akin to shock therapy. While it does appear to have worked, it still could have gone very wrong.

Me: You're talking about the incident with the straight razor.

EC: *Yes. And now that he's done that, he feels relieved of any anxiety that whatever it was that caused his friends' disappearance is still interested in him.*

Me: Do you believe the danger is passed?

EC: *Well, if the Los Sima disappearances are indeed enkanto-related, and you and I both believe that to be true, then at the very least, Gus—given his current physical appearance— would no longer be of any interest to them.*

Me: Are you the only mental health professional that deals with these kinds of specialized cases?

EC: *That I know of, yes.*

Me: And what do your colleagues think of your atypical practice?

EC: *The thing is, only a select few actually know that this is the specialty I've chosen. Even fewer understand, if not completely believe. What none of them can argue with is that I've helped many of my patients adjust to life after experiencing phenomena that just cannot be explained in any rational manner. And a lot of those patients were referrals.*

These were people they found they just could not help. And you and I both know that's because they were approaching the cases as if the experiences that were being recounted were elaborate metaphors for some kind of trauma whose details the patients had first blocked out, then subsequently dressed up in fairy tale and folklore imagery. They would have done more harm if they'd continued to treat these patients in a "normal" manner.

Me: Have you always been a believer?

EC: *No, not really.* [Pauses] *We both agreed that I wouldn't talk about that. At least not now.*

Me: Yes, we did. You don't have to say anything more.

EC: [After a long pause] *You showed me some of the letters that were sent to your publisher. And you were right, there were a lot of accounts in there that were simply not true. I'm sure some of those were people who were punking you for a laugh.*

But it's possible that some others were, as you put it, people who have always been believers, in that this is something they've chosen to believe in because they desperately need to place their belief in something.

They want to believe. In anything. The kinds of people who end up becoming rabid fundamentalists or part of a cult.

In my experience though—again, both professional and personal—you only really believe in these things after you've seen them. After something's happened to you.

You're actually an odd case.

Me: What makes you say that?

EC: *Well, you haven't really seen anything, right? Seen something when it was close enough to touch. I mean, I know you've seen specimens and physical evidence, carcasses…*

Me: I've seen a carcass. And it was badly decomposed, so I didn't touch it. And then the local authorities promptly "lost" it while in transit. And I've seen a couple of skeletons. Those I touched. A bit.

EC: *All right. Skeletons and a single badly-rotted carcass. But you haven't seen one alive, have you? Right in front of you, breathing on you…*

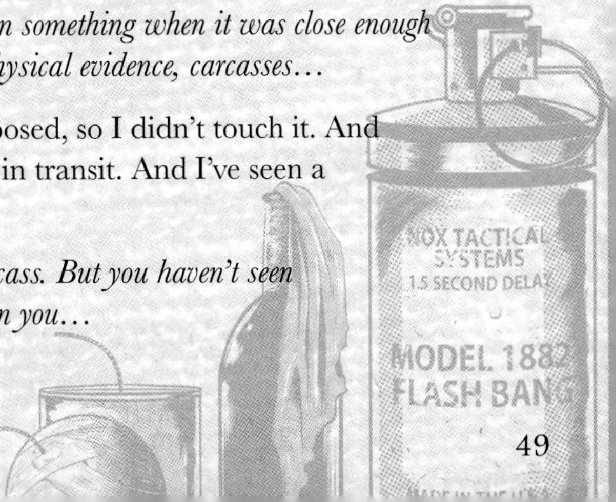
SYSTEMS

Me: No. And I don't want to.

EC: *Of course not. No one in their right mind should want to. But see, even though you've yet to experience something first-hand, the way Gus has, you already believe. Through osmosis, let's say. But trust me, if you do see one of them—and it really won't matter what kind—you'll become a believer of a whole different sort.*

Me: Just so long as you'll welcome me into the club.

EC: [Laughs] *Oh, wholeheartedly. Drinks will be on me. And the morning after, once our hangovers have passed, we can have our very first session.*

Me: [*Laughs*] All right. For the record, if someone were to ask you, "What exactly do you mean by 'supranormal trauma'?", what would your answer be?

EC: *I usually have two answers to that.*
    The first is, it's essentially post-traumatic stress disorder. It's PTSD, where the event that caused it is one that involved supernatural elements.
    My second go-to answer is one I use if I know the person asking is a fan of horror films.

Me: Oh, okay. Go.

EC: *You know the kind of horror movie where it's a family, with kids, maybe a family pet, and all that frightening horror movie stuff happens to them?*
    I first had this thought in high school, when I got to see Poltergeist. The first, original one. We leave the family in that Holiday Inn, and by the way, I was so happy the dog survived…

Me: Yay, E. Buzz!

EC: *…the hauntingly beautiful music starts—*

Me: I love that soundtrack! Jerry Goldsmith! Sorry.

EC: [Laughs] *No, that's okay. I do, too. So, the music's there, and the end credits start to roll, and I thought, 'Wow. Those kids are going to need years of therapy to get straightened out.'*

Me: [*Laughs*] And that was rated PG, on appeal. There are some movies out there like you're talking about that were released with an R rating! Those movies' kids will need even more therapy!

EC: *Because it isn't enough to just survive something like that. You also need to survive with your sanity, if not intact, then at least in some kind of manageable, working order.* [Pause]

The troubling thing about it is, nothing in an R-rated horror film can really compare to an actual first-hand experience. It's terror that's bone deep…that's gut deep. It fills you up till you feel like you're drowning in it… [Long pause]

Me: There was…one patient in particular you mentioned before…that you could also talk about a little?

EC: *Yes…Yes. I feel this patient's recovery will be helped tremendously by getting her experience out there.*

Me: But there's a hurdle to that.

EC: *Not from me, I can assure you. But they seem to be leaning towards giving me a "Yes." Just as soon as they're fairly certain they can monetize the entire thing.*

Me: Maybe we should start-

EC: *Yes, I'm so sorry.*
While we can't talk about the incident yet, I can give you the barest hint of a gist, and for that, let's start at the beginning.

The patient I'm talking about is a writer. Let's call her "X."
X started out her career writing romance novels. You know the kind, I'm sure. The ones with shirtless male models with long, flowing hair on their covers. She was making a decent living, but it was when she decided to write a horror novel that her career really took off.

Of course, at the time, a woman writing a horror novel—particularly one whose name was already associated with romance novels—was something the marketing people didn't know what to do with. So that horror novel, the one that started it all, was released under a pseudonym. A male pseudonym.

And when that novel sold big and the demand for a follow-up was insistent, her manager and her agent decided the best course of action for everyone concerned was to keep up the ruse.

If ever she wanted to write another romance novel, she was free to do so, but if she was going to write a horror novel—and the consensus was, she should, because that single horror novel sold far more copies than her four romance novels combined—she would need to use the pseudonym. And so she did. She wrote many more horror novels.

And she and her "team" and her publisher all became rich, and all that money was tied into that pseudonym.

You've read "his" novels. That pseudonym is a household name when it comes to horror. They're the kinds of novels you see people reading on airplanes or beaches. The kinds of horror novels Hollywood adapts because of the brand recognition.

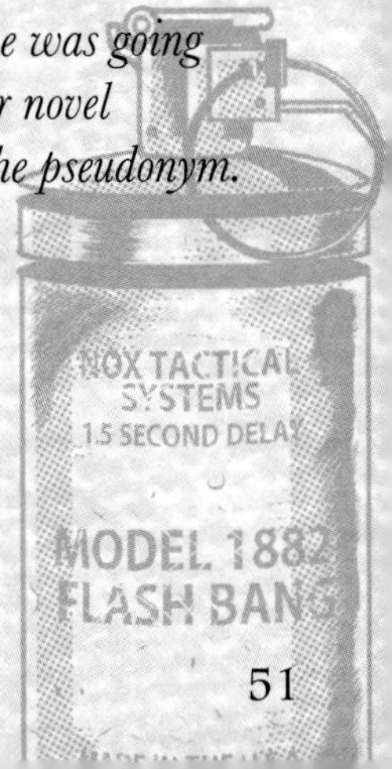

NOX TACTICAL
SYSTEMS
1.5 SECOND DELA
MODEL 188
FLASH BAN

Me: And the author's picture on the jackets? The public appearances and readings? The signings and talk shows?

EC: *A hired actor. There was a time they had to shell out a ridiculous amount of money to keep videos of some auditions he'd done in the past off the market.*

Me: So some people know that it's all a scam.

EC: *Of course. It's one of those industry "secrets" that people shut up about because vast sums of money are rolling in.*
Which is why, when it happened, they just got ghost writers to keep the books coming.

Me: And by "it," you mean…

EC: *The incident that caused her an unbelievable amount of supranormal trauma.*
She just shut down. And as far as the publisher was concerned, it couldn't have happened at a worse time. They were sympathetic to what they believed was some kind of "breakdown," but deadlines for the next book—the fourth installment in what was originally presented as a trilogy—were fast approaching, and the manuscript was far from complete.
So damage control meant getting a ghost writer to finish and polish, and wouldn't you know it, this one sold even more than the third, which already broke all kinds of records.
Meanwhile, X was very, very slowly making a recovery.

Me: And were you already treating her at this time?

EC: *No, not yet. But she was a referral. A close colleague of mine felt he couldn't do anything more for her, so he sent her my way.*

Me: And you were able to help her.

EC: *Enough that she started to communicate again. But of course, everything is now filtered through a third person lens. She can now only talk about her experience as if it were a story, and she was a character in that story.*

Me: And you were the one who convinced her to write that letter to me, because you felt it would help her.

EC: *Yes, and it has. She's talking about other things now, still in the third person, but at least, she's communicating about things other than just that one, horrible experience she had.*
You remember, you told me when we first met that the reason X's account stood out was because of those other accounts that were written in the third person.

Me: Yeah. With X, there was your cover letter, that explained why I was about to read a first-person account in the third person. The others were just stories that were written in the third person. How am I supposed to take that seriously as a personal experience?

So then it was you I did my research on, because the story about the female romance writer-turned-horror novelist under a male pseudonym was really just so out there, I had to make sure there were people involved who weren't wackadoo.

And you certainly weren't. Like you said, even the other psychologists I talked to who really don't believe couldn't say anything against your success rate.

EC: *Of course, "success" is a very relative term in the mental health field. Because we're all really just going at this one day at a time, aren't we? Even me. Some patients, like Gus, emerge from the trauma surprisingly well-adjusted.*

But I have other patients, like X, who need a whole lot of professional care, and time, in order to come out the other side as a reasonably functioning human being.

Me: You know, I really did want to run X's account in the Black Bestiary.

EC: *You and me both. But like I said, the publisher seems to be coming around. Their marketing people seem to think they can release the account as a novel, or at the very least, a novella.*

Me: Under the pseudonym?

EC: *Oh, no. They'd release it under yet another pseudonym. We can only hope it'll at least be a female pseudonym this time. It's their hope that X will continue to write afterwards, so they can get her back in the game, so to speak.*

Me: Do you think that's possible?

EC: *I hope so, if only so that she can have that choice again. To function in that manner. After what happened to her, the state she was in… She may as well have been catatonic.*

When she started to communicate in the third person… It was like she'd come back to life. She was engaging with the world again.

That's what I want for all my patients. That they can re-enter the world again, even after knowing what's out there in the dark.

If they can be proactive about it, like Gus, who's now been taken under R.J.'s wing and is working hard to wean himself off the drugs and the alcohol, then that's wonderful. That's more than I'd hope for for many of the people who've come under my care.

I just want them to stand up again, to not be destroyed by whatever it was that brushed up so disastrously against them.

NOX TACTICAL
SYSTEMS

MODEL 1882
FLASH BANG

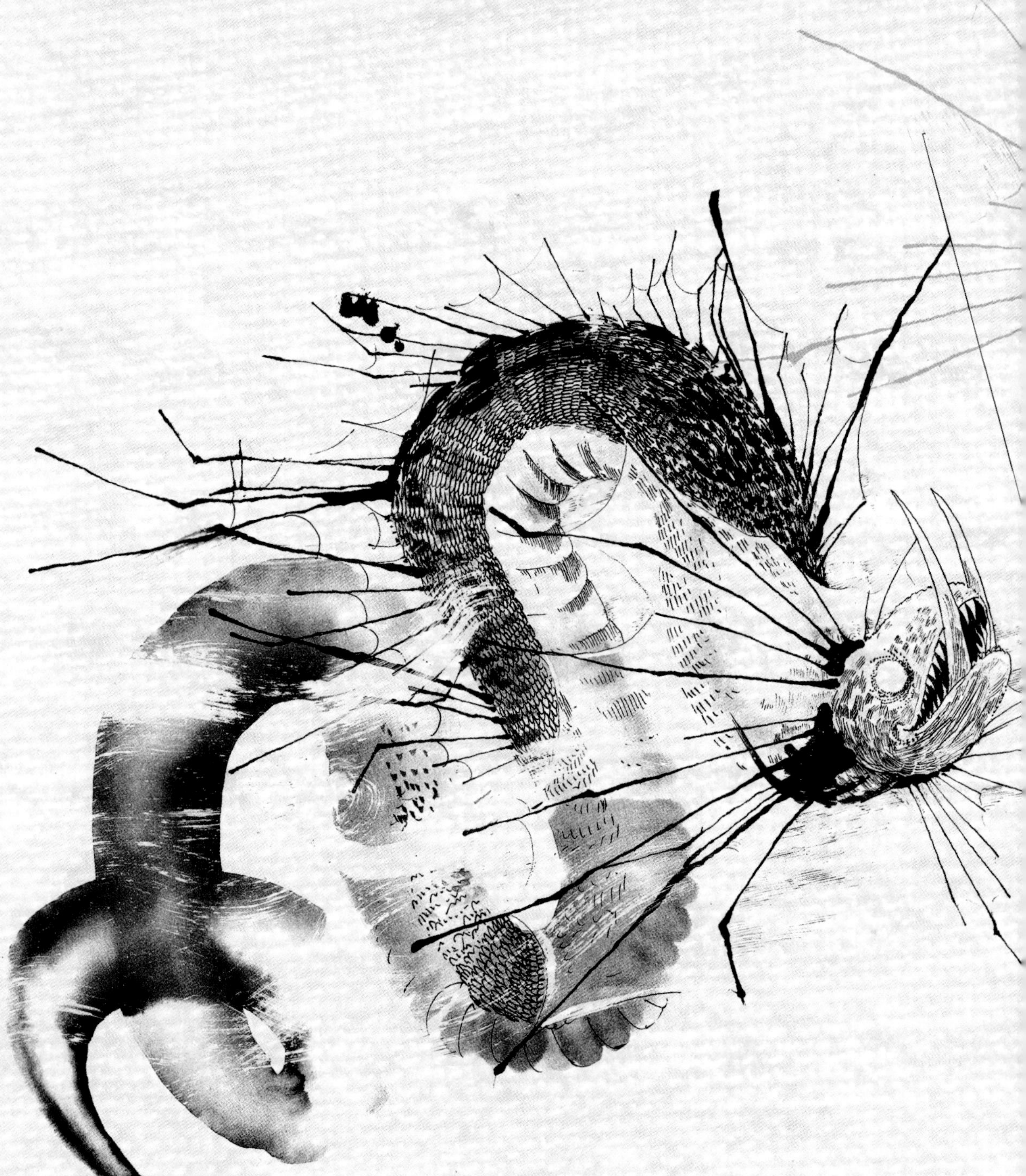

MAMELEU

Fishermen of Laguna Bay fear the "burning pools of water" which supposedly appear during the nights of the full moon. If fishermen venture too far from their usual fishing grounds, they sometimes enter an area where the water turns blood red and a fiery light appears under their boat.

The unlucky fishermen who don't turn back immediately are eaten by the *Mameleu*, a giant sea serpent with two, large round eyes that burn with eldritch fire. Its eyes allow it to see and explore the deepest part of the ocean.

It uses its 18-foot long tusks to attack boats and ships, overturning them and making the crew fall overboard.

There have been foolish attempts to try and hunt and kill the *Mameleu*. The unfortunate crew would either get swallowed whole or suffer a more painful death when the *Mameleu* spits out its green venom, which burns the skin and makes one's organs explode.

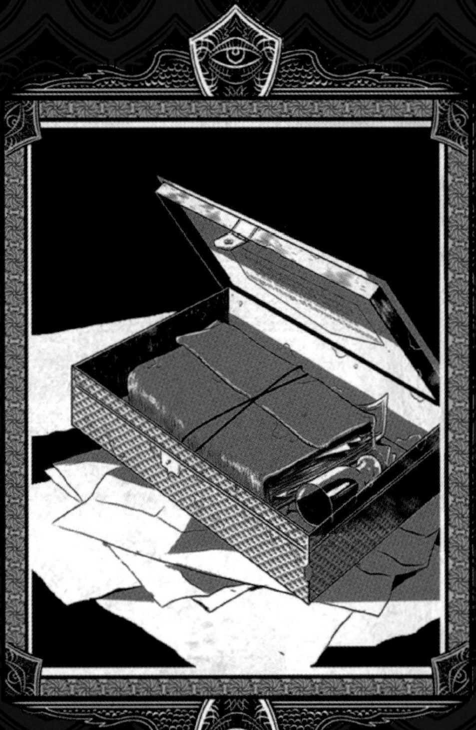

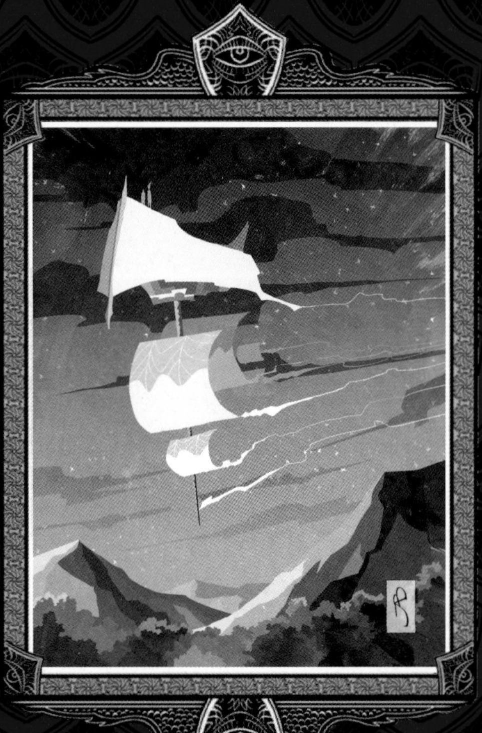

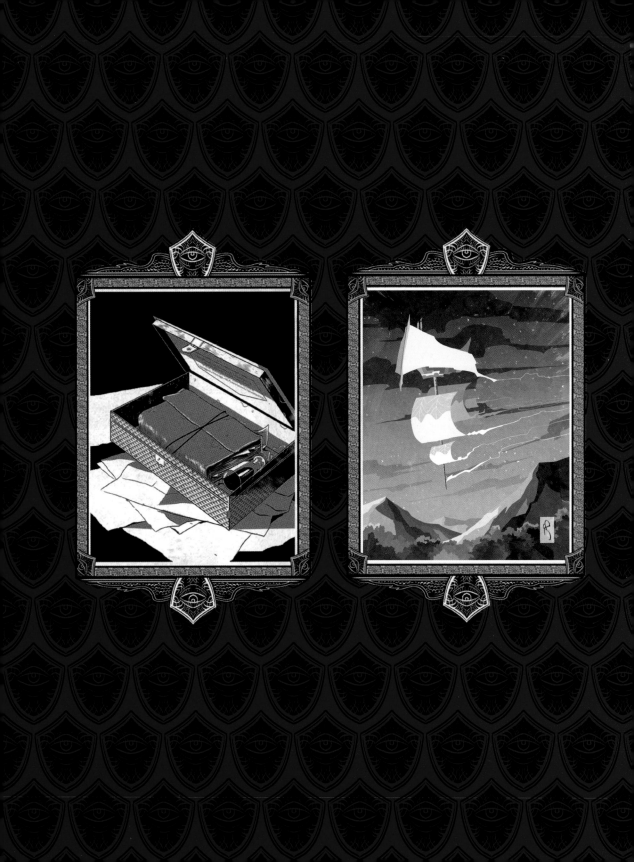

STANISLAV
SWALLOW THE "MOOT-YA"

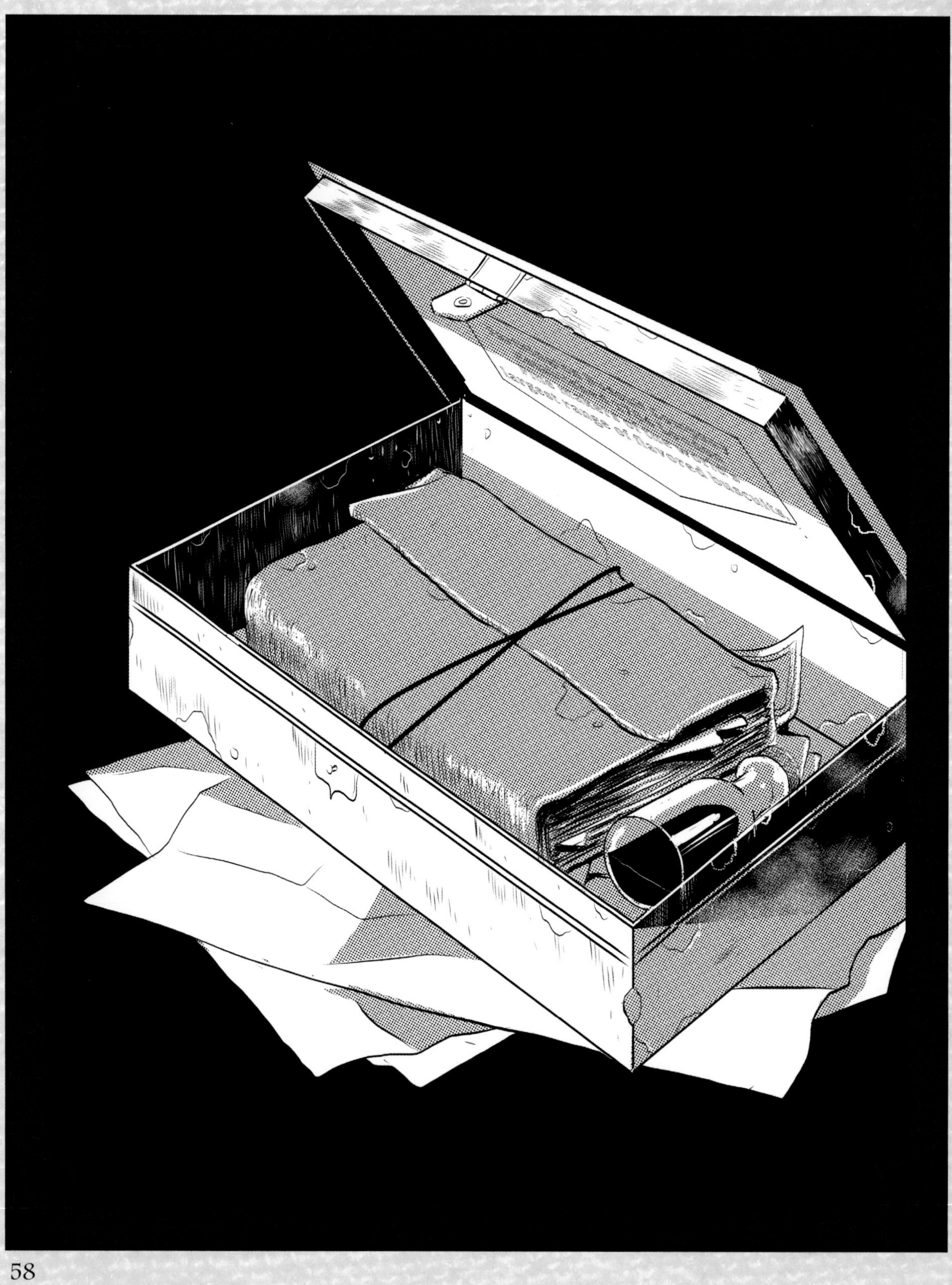
largest range of flavored biscuits

My name is Stanislav. When I was young, in Estonia, my nickname was "Stasik," but now, many people just call me "Stan."

I grew up in Tallinn, where we speak Russian, and it was only when I was 14 and we move to Germany that I begin to speak English, because I met an American girl there, in Frankfurt, where some of our family first move in early 1990's.

I learn little German there, but English, a *lot*. Because of Millie, not just because she teach me, but also because we spend time together and she make me talk and talk and talk in English.

But some days, it is still like something new to me, English. It is very confusing, sometimes.

We move to Frankfurt, many of my family. *Moi roditeli*… uhhh, my *parents*. Yes. And my one sister and three brothers. And *moy dyadya*. My uncle, Yefim.

We move to Frankfurt so *dyadya* could be close to his other…siblings? Like other brothers and sisters? *Dyadya* was sick with the cancer, but he was fighting. Still, the doctors did not know how long before the cancer would win, because they said it would, some day soon. It was… uhhh… terminal?

Before we leave Tallinn, when we were packing, *dyadya* come to my room and hand me a box. He say in Russian, "Pack the box with your things."

I say back to him in Russian, "Pack the box with *your* things, *dyadya*!"

He say, "I am old now, Stasik. I forget. I do not want to forget this box or where I pack it. *You* keep box with *your* things, so we do not forget where it is when we reach Germany. The box is *important*, Stasik."

"And what is in the box, *dyadya*?" I ask.

"History," he say. "Truth."

And I say, "Fine! Give me the box!" and I pack it with my things, and I think, "*Oy, dyadya* is *psikh*!" Like, crazy-loony, yes?

We are in Frankfurt for one week only, and then *dyadya* die. The cancer won.

I miss *moy dyadya*…

I met Millie the day after the *pokhorony*, the… funeral?

I was sad and I missed *dyadya* and I missed my friends in Tallinn, and I went to moon13, so maybe the music would make me forget for a little bit.

My older cousins got me inside, because even if I have always been big for my age, I was only 14.

I saw Millie for the first time when "Islands" was on… you know, by The XX?

[Singing slightly off-key] "I don't have to leave anymore… what I have is right here…"

So much better than the Shakira remake cover. Original *always* better…

I saw her and heard that song, and think, "Yes. She is the girl I want to dance with. She can make me forget all the things I want to forget this night."

So I ask my cousins how to say "Would you like to dance?" in English, and they tell me.

So I go to her, ask her "Would you like to dance?" like big stupid parrot, and she say, "Why not?"

And we dance, and I forget.

For a little bit.

Oy, now I miss Millie…

If she was here, she would keep on fixing my damaged English. Now, no one fixes it. All I speak now is *Eeng-gloosh*. *[Smiles sheepishly]* "Eeng-gloosh" is what Millie calls my shameful broken English.

Sometimes, is *so* bad…

Izvineniya. Sorry.

I think maybe I should stop thinking about Millie and tell my story, but then, if not for Millie, maybe I never find *dyadya's* box again and I would not be here today, telling you my story.

It was months later, months after *dyadya* die, months of talking English with Millie, and going out. When we met in moon13, I tell Millie I am 17, but she see through lie after week or so, so I tell truth, I am 14, even though I look older. So she "go slow" with me, because she is 18 and she does not want to be "cradle snatcher."

So even if we kiss and fool around a little, much of the time it is just talking and talking and talking English.

And one time, she is in my room and looking all over place, in closet and under bed, all over. Because she want to *know* me. And she find *dyadya's* box, at the back of closet, behind new pair of sneakers.

She ask, "What's this?"

And I say, "Oh, box left by *dyadya*."

And she make that funny face I love when I say Russian word that she does not understand. So I say, "*Dyadya*. My mother's brother."

"Uncle," she say, and this first time I ever hear the word.

Uncle.

I say, "I met you in club the day after we bury him."

And Millie look so sad then, and she return the box to back of closet, and come over to me, and let me cry like big baby on her shoulder.

I finally look in box a week later, and inside is very old journal, many of it worn and torn and falling apart. Crumbling? Is that right? Many pages filled with writing, and some pages with drawings, but many of the drawings were very much destroyed. Also, old-looking test tube with liquid inside, and a letter.

A letter from *dyadya*, for me.

In letter, *dyadya* say again how important box is, and he say that I am to be the keeper of box now, that I should keep it safe, and that I should touch the *flakon*—the word he use in his letter for the test tube—once a year, on my birthday. Is "vial" in English, *flakon*.

He say this very important, and I should not forget. Touch *flakon*, and one day, something would happen, he did not know what, but it would be out of ordinary, and when that happens, that I should swallow what is in *flakon*.

And again, I think *dyadya* really is *psikh*! Who knows how long that liquid is in *flakon*, yeah? Who knows even *what* liquid is? Maybe it poison, or maybe it good before but after such a long time it now turn to poison…

But in letter, *dyadya* say this very important, not just to our family, but to the world.

So I do what *dyadya* say. I make it my tradition. Every year, on my birthday, I open box and I touch *flakon*. It is like me going to cemetery to visit *dyadya*. As… reminder? No…

Ahh! Remembrance!

Yes.

Remembrance.

So I do that, every year, on my birthday.

Sometimes, I read the journal, but it look very old and I worry it will just one day crumble in my hands into nothing, so I do not do that a lot.

It is the *flakon* I focus on.

Every year. On my birthday.

And for three years, is same. Open box, touch *flakon*, remember *dyadya*, return *flakon*, close box. Every year, same.

Until last year, on my 17th birthday, when the *flakon glow*, like there is fire inside it, and then I see that it is not liquid inside anymore, but something *solid*, and burning with that glow.

Like a *jewel.*

And then I hear voice, not *dyadya's* voice, and voice say I need to swallow the jewel.

Voice call the jewel a *"moot-ya."*

As I was going through Stanislav's account for the first time, sensing where his words were taking me, anticipating whose journal that was that had been left for him by his late uncle, foremost in my mind was this thought: If this is true, this is going to be the centerpiece of the follow-up.

Not only was this new information, but it was new information that served to bolster things already established in the LJ.

Once I finished reading the account, I knew my first order of business was to go back to the research we'd done for the LJ, those avenues where we were trying to find living descendants to any of the three artists who'd accompanied Pardo on his journeys. Avenues that had ultimately hit dead ends.

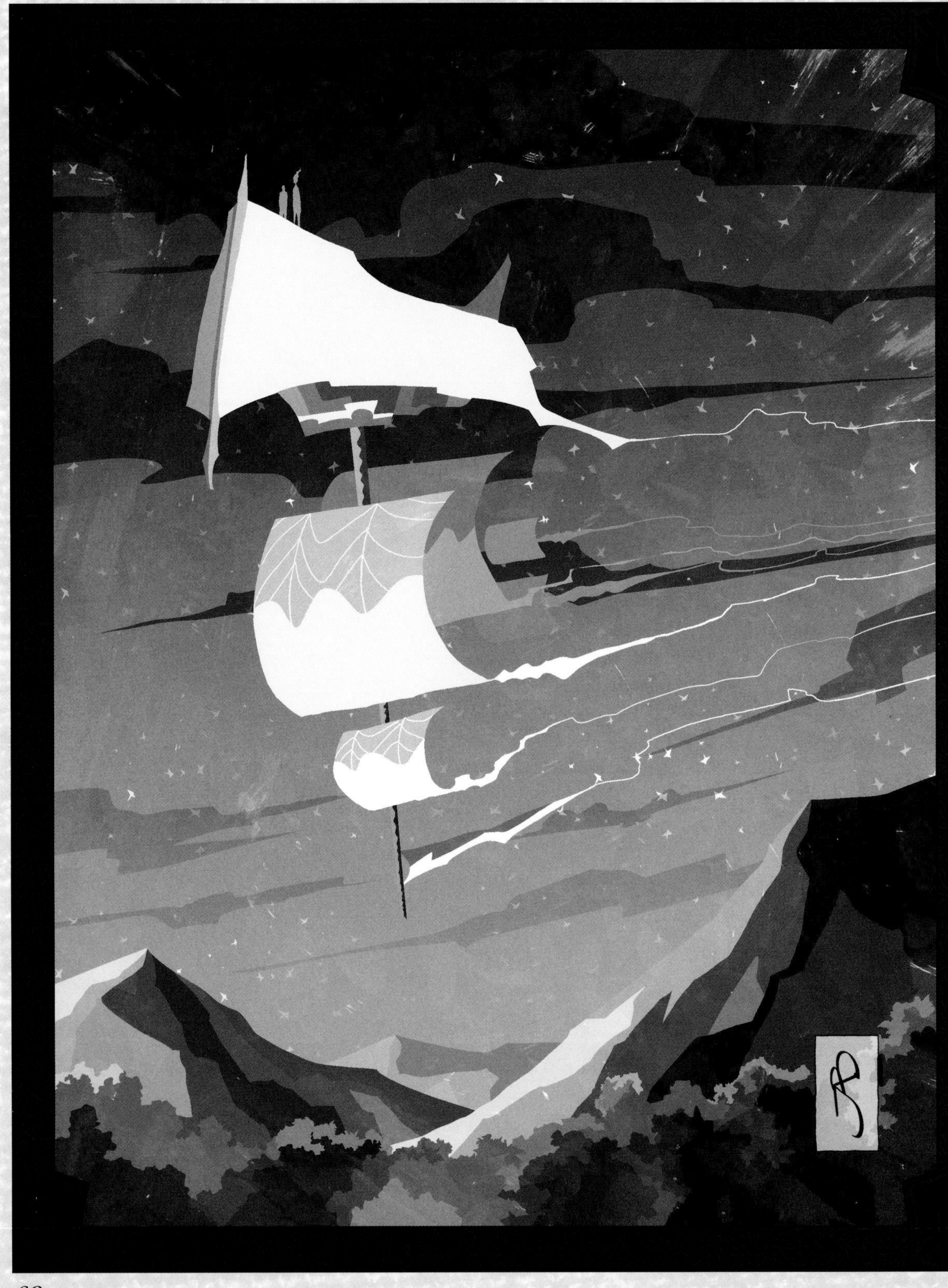

At the same time, I began to make tentative overtures to Stanislav, particularly to any of his older relatives who would be willing to go on record and speak to me about their family history or share any diaries or journals from their deceased relatives. I quickly began to see why we had initially hit dead ends.

It turns out that Stanislav's family has changed surnames at key points in the past, most recently in 1992, in the wake of the dissolution of the Soviet Union, and Stanislav's family splintered across several countries, each group taking on a new surname.

But the link was cut as early as the 19th century, as we will see later.

Once I was fairly certain of the legitimacy of Stanislav's account, I was given access to the journal left by his late uncle, and as he described in his account, it was weathered and practically disintegrating. (It pained me to see the document in such a state, and I wondered vainly what was now forever lost to us.)

While Pardo seldom mentioned his compatriots, and even more rarely in any great detail, they were more clearly depicted in this journal, which I would discover once belonged to Stanislav's ancestor, Kolya. (The other two artists who accompanied Pardo were Asif, who was of Middle Eastern descent, and Marisol, a mestiza born in the Philippines.)

While Kolya's journal does not mention the incident specifically, it can be deduced that Kolya came to be indebted to Pardo when the latter helped his family deal with an "extramundane" problem.

It was thus Kolya's way of paying off that debt by accompanying Pardo to be one of his "ocular chroniclers," given that the Russian was clearly an artist of no small talent.

It is telling that when Kolya left his family, not only did the family change their surname, but Kolya himself took another surname as well.

It is never overtly addressed in Kolya's journal, but my assumption here is, whatever "extramundane" troubles Pardo helped Kolya's family with, it still cast a shadow over them, so much so that they felt the need to change their surname, as if in an attempt to erase their family from history.

And so I swallowed the jewel. The "*moot-ya*."

And at first, nothing happen. I wait for something, even if that something is me dropping like dead fly because jewel was poison after all.

I am just about to curse *dyadya* again for being *psikh* because nothing happen, when I *feel* it. Like warm feeling, all over my body, in my muscles and my bones. It spread, like I step into tub full of warm water.

I feel strong then, like I am Superman, yeah? Like Hulk!

And I think, next, I will get crazy-cool costume and have my walk in slow motion towards camera, like in the superhero movies.

But I get voice instead. *Another* voice. A woman's voice. And she say she will now fulfill her promise, and suddenly, *whoooosh!*

At first, I think I am flying now, like Superman, but then I see I am in boat of light. And the boat is sailing not in the sea, but in the sky! In the clouds!

Not as cool as being Superman, but cool enough.

Then I think I am on drugs! That is it! The "*moot-ya*" was not poison, but *drugs!*

I never get high on drugs before, so I think maybe this is how it is.

It was *like* a dream, but I was not dreaming because I was awake, but still I was in the dream, but it was also very real. That make no sense, I know, but that is what it feel like.

Then I hear the voice again, the woman, and I turn around and there she is, standing beside me on the boat of light!

She say many, many things, the woman.

She say she know who I am, and that she help me now because my family help her before, and this was the same boat as before, and blah blah blah.

She talk and talk and talk, *worse* than Millie, because Millie slow down and then stay quiet and let *me* talk, and fix my Eeng-gloosh if I am wrong. The woman, she just go on and on and on.

One of the many, many things she say, she say I should write letter, and in letter I should tell my story, *this* story.

And I say who will I write letter to?

And she say, write letter first, and when I am finished, I will know who I should send letter to.

Then I wake up.

But not in my bed, not in my room, not in house in Frankfurt.

I wake up in Brighton Beach in Brooklyn! In New York, United States!

I am in house of my cousin, my cousin who live in Brooklyn.

And I do not know how I got there!

I call home first, because I know *mama* will be crazy when I tell her where I am, but she just laugh because she say of *course* I am in Brooklyn, because I ask to come here to visit *kuzen* Pavel. She tell me to be safe and that she need to go to help my sister Tamara and she hang up.

And I think maybe I am the one who is now crazy, because of course I do not remember any of what she say!

How do I forget trip from Germany to United States?! The only flying I remember is on that bright boat of light!

I think, yes, I am now definitely *psikh* like *dyadya*.

And I remember I am supposed to write letter, so you know what? I *do*. I write letter, because if I am now the one who is crazy, then I will *double down* on the crazy, yeah? That what they say when you bet, right? "Double down"?

That is what I do. I double down.

I write letter, and when I finish, I hear voice again. First voice, the one that tell me to swallow the "*moot-ya.*" Voice tell me address. *Your* address. The address of your publisher.

I have no idea who you are or who your publisher is or about your book.

I just listen to voice, write down address, and send letter.

Then I try and enjoy Brighton Beach, even though I am still scared and worried about how I got there…

And so I read Stanislav's written account, and trying to manage my expectations, made initial contact, and began to interview his older relatives.

Once everything began to fall into place, and the veracity of his story was determined, it was mutually agreed upon that Stanislav was safest if he moved into the compound as well.

Before we move on to the journal itself, there are two points of interest regarding Stanislav that I'd like to take a look at.

One: the circumstances of his journey from Frankfurt to New York, and two: the effects the *mutya* has had on him. (And for those of you passingly familiar with the *mutya*, we will be returning to the apparently atypical nature of how it came to be ingested by Stanislav in the section entitled "A Closer Look at Kolya's Journal.")

∽∾ THE BOAT OF LIGHT ∾∽

Now, while Stanislav's account of being a passenger on a flying "boat of light" has some characteristics common to tales of faerie abduction (particularly the presence of a kind of supranatural vessel—as per the "burning chariots" sometimes used by faeries—as well as Stanislav's sense of missing time), I feel the pertinent question here is, how exactly did Stanislav travel from Germany to the US?

Did he travel via supranatural vessel, as per his memories, or via plane, as per the statements of his relatives?

My supposition here is, both.

I believe that Stanislav's spirit or soul was taken on the boat of light so the mysterious woman could speak with him and impart some of the knowledge he required, while his physical body, operating on a kind of autopilot, went through the mundane motions of passport and visa and airliner, and once his body arrived safely in Brighton Beach and the woman had divulged whatever information she needed to, Stanislav's two halves were reunited.

Which was when he "awoke" and realized he was no longer in Frankfurt.

While the "boat of light" may also superficially resemble the flying ships of the *dalakitnon* (see LJ), it is difficult to make any kind of solid conjecture without knowing the true nature of the mysterious woman.

In a follow-up session with Stanislav, I tried to have him recall as much of what was told to him by the woman as he could.

I also pressed him as to the woman's appearance, but interestingly, Stanislav could not seem to remember exactly what she looked like.

I'm making an inference here, but I think Stanislav refers to the individual as a female only because he received the impression that he was interacting with a feminine presence, and not necessarily because it was an actual woman he was conversing with.

Since several of the creatures profiled in the LJ have the ability to disguise themselves under a false appearance, it isn't such a huge leap to suggest that Stanislav could have been talking to anything on that ship.

——◇ THE MUTYA ◇——

As best as R.J. can determine, Stanislav has indeed become the recipient of heightened levels of physical strength and endurance. Though there has been no opportunity to actually test just how much stronger and more physically resilient he has become, R.J. estimates that given his current strength levels, Stanislav would have no trouble facing a *kapre* or a *tikbalang*, if he needed to.

I just hope that when the time comes, Stanislav will be prepared.

As much as he is clearly excited about the vaguely absurd—though admittedly poignant and oddly hopeful—prospect of a superhero codename and costume, he's really just an 18-year-old boy (which, of course, explains the excitement).

He may look like he's in his mid-20's, but he's still a teenager, and yes, he's experienced some strangeness, but he has yet to come face to face with any beast from the LJ.

Right now, trading punches with a *kapre* is purely a theoretical scenario for him, like something out of a comic book or a movie, an attitude R.J. is trying to dislodge so he can be better prepared for such an eventuality.

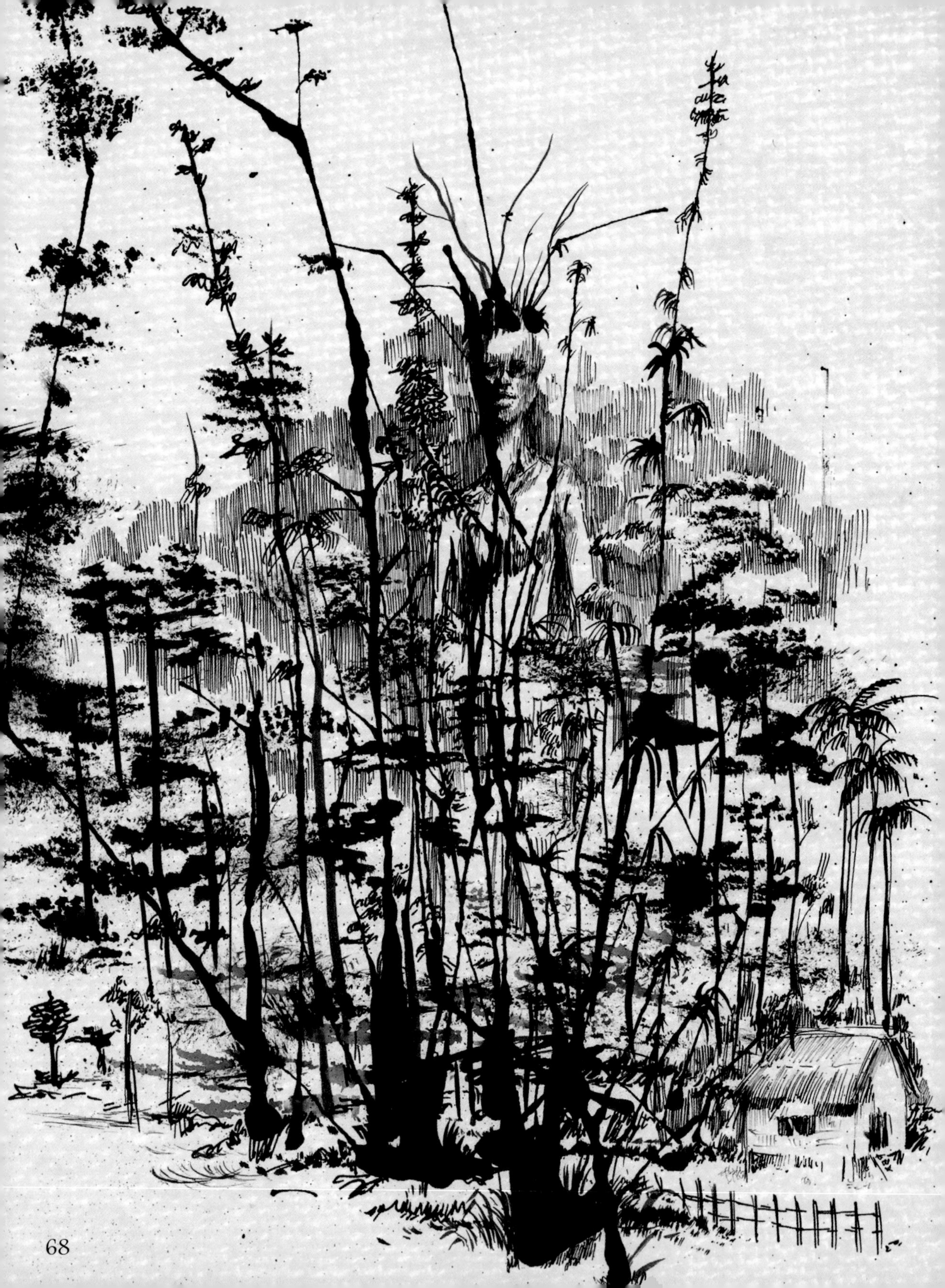

MANTIW

As the story goes, farmers were surprised to find a young man stranded on top of the tallest coconut tree in the land. The man claims he had been yelling for help for nearly a week, but no one could hear his cries for assistance.

He was supposedly snatched by an angry giant, which was later identified as a *Mantiw*.

He earned the *Mantiw's* anger because he serenaded the beautiful daughter of the haciendero.

The daughter claimed that a shy and mysterious stranger had been whistling the most beautiful tunes to her at night. Looking out her window, she saw nobody, but swore the tune was coming from the field of coconut trees.

The young man heard the story and said he could sing better than the shy stranger. He went to the haciendero's daughter and whistled his best tune. His performance got him an invitation to have dinner with the family. After dinner, he bid them farewell and headed home. He never made it back.

Six days later, he was found on top of that coconut tree.

He described the *Mantiw* as a dark man, who was as tall as the trees and had a hooked nose and thick lips. These spirit giants protect the fields and trees, commonly seen around coconut and buri palm trees. The *Mantiw* take pride in their whistling skills and are offended when people try to whistle along with them.

Other encounters with the giant claim that the *Mantiw's* whistling can affect the growth of plants and trees; that the more they whistle, the better the vegetation will grow in that area.

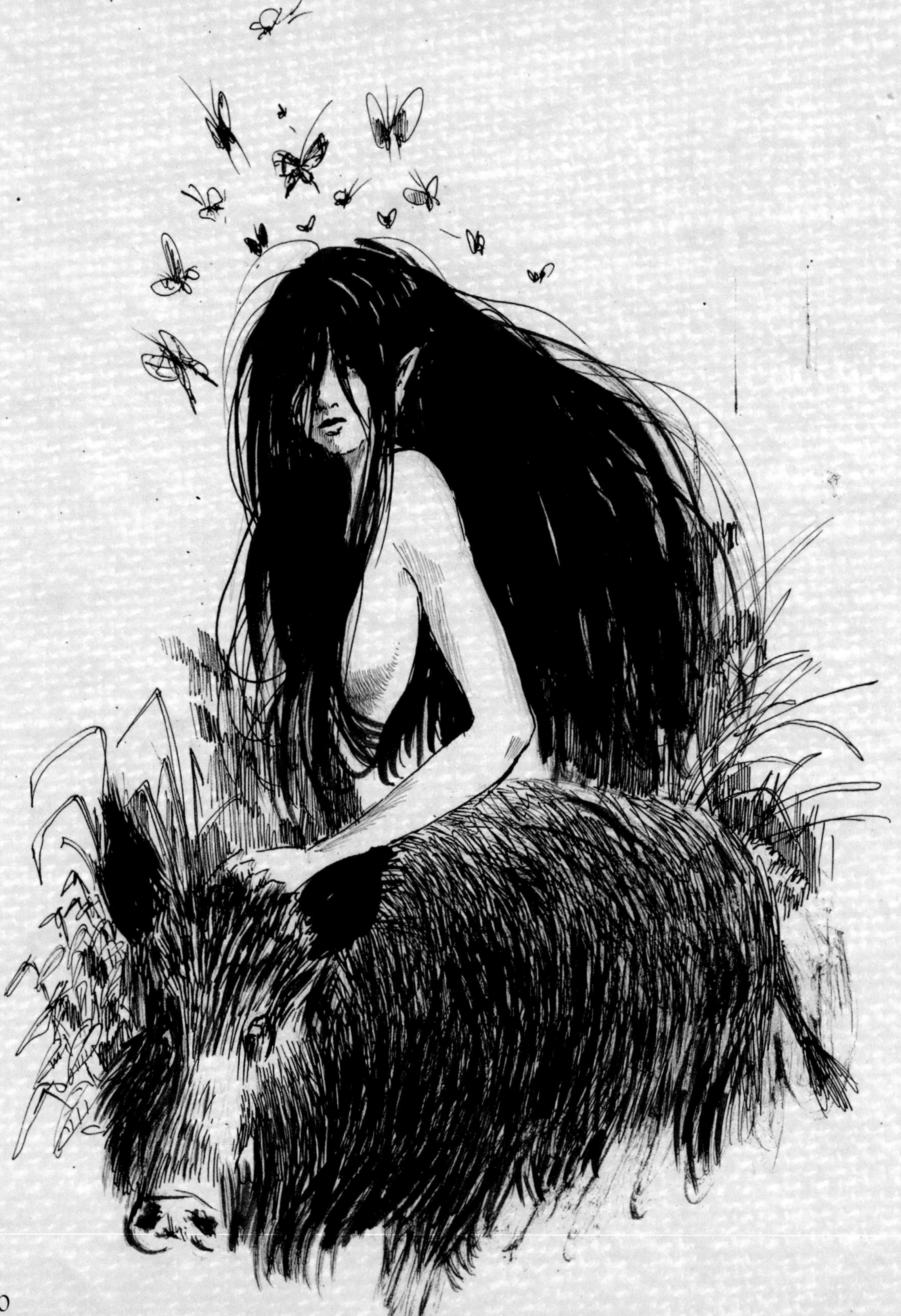

TAHAMALING

Whenever the Bagobo tribe go hunting, they need to ask permission from the maiden of the forest, else the hunters will suffer a terrible illness. The elven maidens, known as the *Tahamaling*, are worshipped by the animals. The animals bring them food, and in return, the *Tahamaling* makes sure no harm comes to them.

There was one witness who said he came upon a beautiful woman with red skin. He could not see her face because of the long, golden hair that covered her face. She was surrounded by deer, wolves, and wild boars, who formed a protective circle around her. Birds and butterflies flew around her like a multicolored halo.

The hunter made the mistake of lifting his weapon, as if to open fire, and the *Tahamaling* ordered the animals to attack. He survived by throwing away his weapon and by pleading for mercy.

The *Tahamaling* is also known to find a lifemate from the *Mahomanay*, the elven tribe that protects the trees and plants of the forest.

We were truly fortunate to have a Bagobo guide who knew the prayers and offerings that needed to be made to appease the *Tahamaling*. The crimson maiden gave us safe passage through her forest. And when we found the lair of the aswang that abducted our companion, the *Tahamaling* came to our rescue by sending her wild pack to protect us.

I was about to thank her with a kiss when one of her wild boars rammed me down, which goes to show that one should always ask permission before kissing a lady.

A. Pardo

71

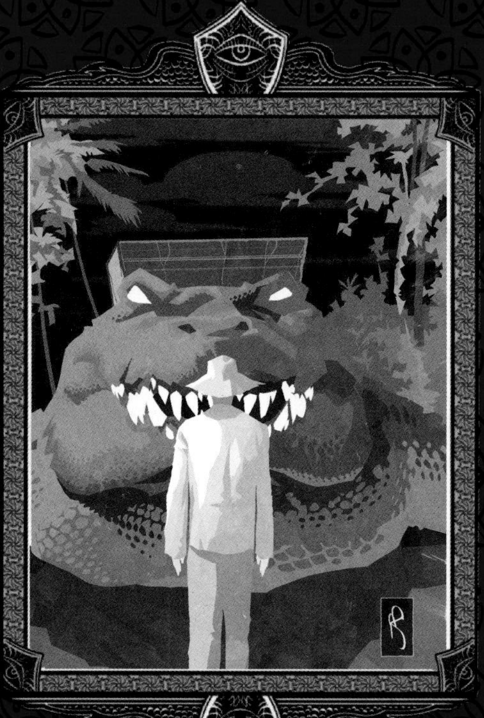

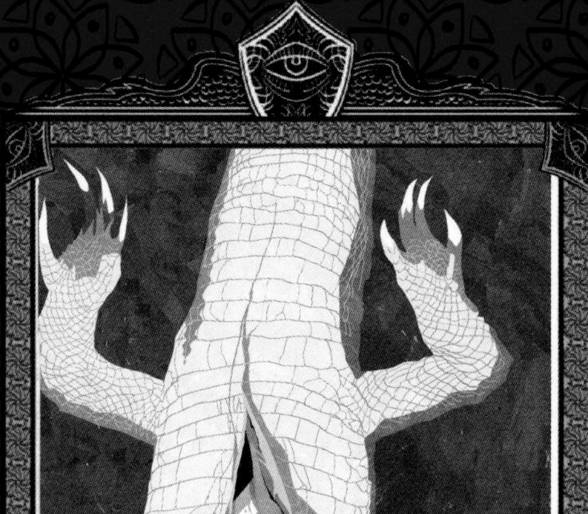

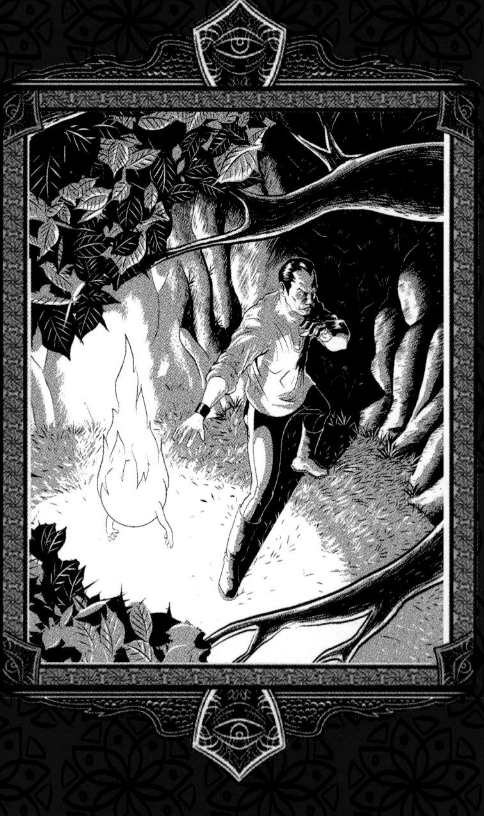

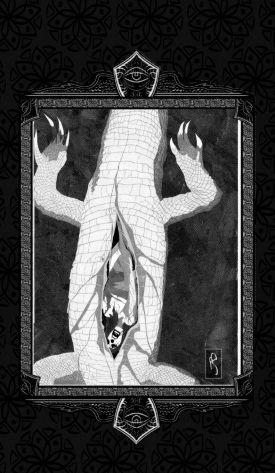

A CLOSER LOOK AT
KOLYA'S JOURNAL

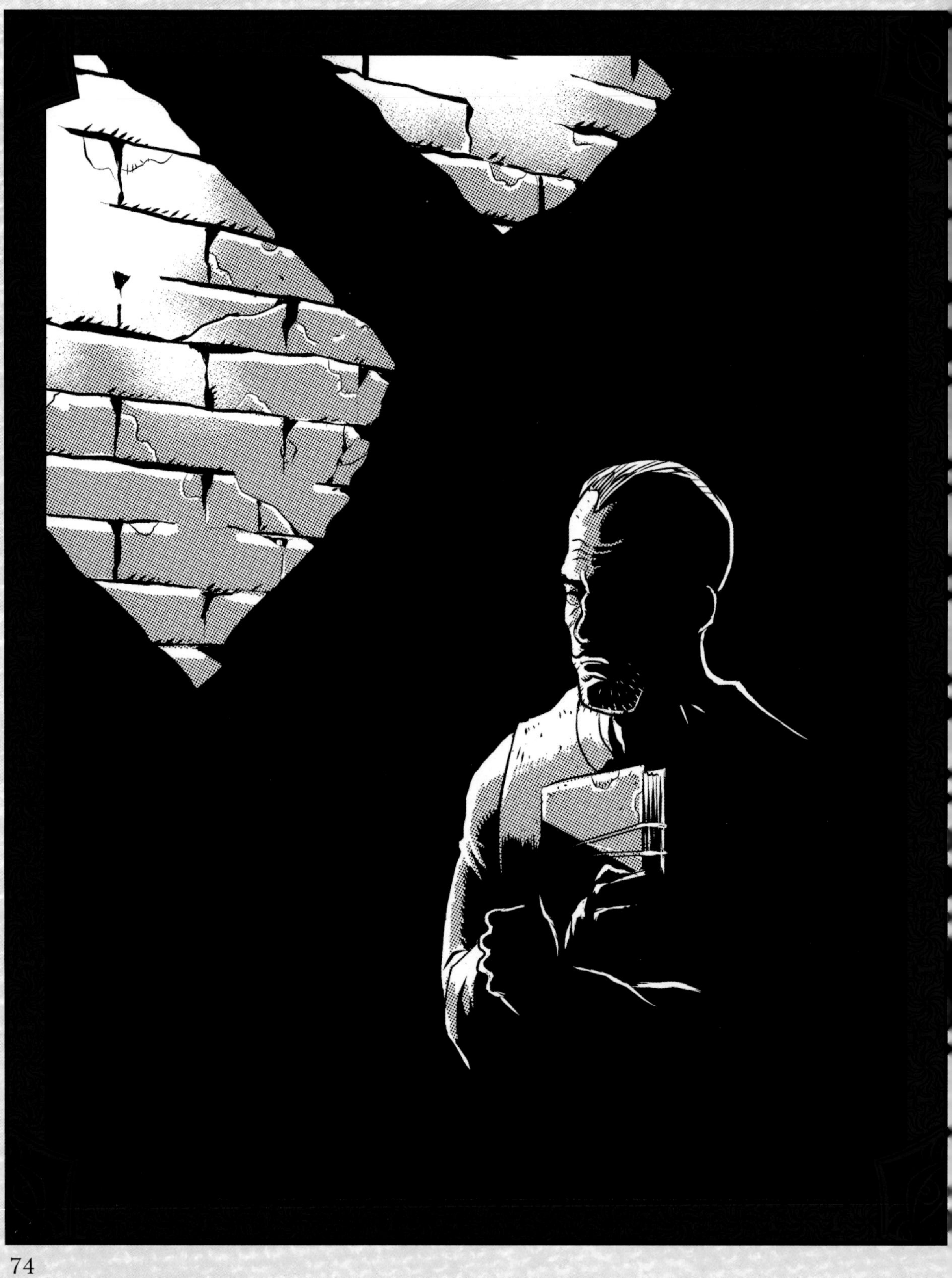

As soon as I laid eyes on the state of Kolya's journal, I knew the first order of business was to scan it in its entirety. That alone was an operation that required a delicate hand, so as to still try and preserve, as best we could, the actual physical document.

Once the journal was scanned, it was then inspected by a number of experts, in an attempt to verify its provenance.

A battery of tests—which included paper and ink analysis, and radiography—was conducted, and the results pointed to the journal having been written sometime in the early to mid-19th century, which does synch up with the period of time Pardo was journeying through the Philippines, as well as the dated entries.

It's interesting to note that the state of Kolya's journal was so markedly different from the scanned appearance of the Pardo Chronicles (PC), if we are to accept the fact that they were both written during the same time period.

Either the PC was written on paper of *much* better stock or extraordinary measures were taken to preserve the document itself.

If I were to hazard a guess, I'd say both.

Sadly, while there were illustrations throughout the journal, most of the pages that suffered the most degradation due to ink corrosion were those that contained Kolya's art, as well as a significant portion of its latter sections (see "The Non-Ending of Kolya's Journal; or, An Appointment Fulfilled").

The tests indicated that the reason was an unidentified component of the iron gall ink used by Kolya. This ingredient appears to have made the ink even more acidic than usual. This, coupled with the less than ideal quality of the journal's paper, contributed to the severe damage.

While most of the written entries were still legible, the illustrations were too far gone for any kind of proper reproduction.

Thus, while it frustrates me that not being able to showcase Kolya's first-person depictions and visual impressions pushes us back a step from the truth we have taken pains to champion, this was the best option, given the circumstances.

The illustrations presented in this section are either reconstructions based on some of the less-damaged illustrations, or interpretations based on Kolya's written entries.

﹋﹏ THE KEEPER ﹏﹌

One of the things Kolya's journal fails to tell us is how exactly the tradition of "the Keeper" came to pass. ("The Keeper" being the term Stanislav's uncle used in the letter he left for his nephew.)

Clearly, it was never a formal office, given the state of deterioration that was allowed to set in on the journal. It seems more a fly-by-the-seat-of-your-pants operation, one that apparently relied quite heavily on circumstance and opportunity.

What follows is what I could piece together from interviews and conversations with several members from different generations of Stanislav's family.

There was always apparently at least one of them in each generation: the odd one, the one who did not seem to fit in, and in most cases, did not seem to want to.

For anyone who's part of a sprawling family, that's a given. I'm sure you've got that weirdo cousin or that bizarro uncle. Sometimes, it's someone from your family unit, your father, or your younger sister.

Maybe it's even you.

But maybe those outliers have a secret, maybe they're a "Keeper," with a secret stash that includes a journal written by an ancestor long gone, and a magic jewel called a *mutya*.

At this point, it's impossible to know who Kolya chose to be the first Keeper, but we have to presume he passed the journal and the *mutya* on to someone he trusted.

We have to presume that he also passed along the instructions regarding the *mutya*.

Time and generations of the family passed, and the journal and the *mutya* moved forward as well, from one Keeper to another, an odd and mysterious inheritance.

Given the scarcity of information that we have, anything might have happened.

It's possible that in some generations, there was more than just one Keeper.

Perhaps the Keeper might also have been gifted with powers like those Kolya had.

All we know for certain is that, eventually, the journal and the *mutya* came into the hands of Stanislav's uncle, Yefim.

﹋﹏ THE TRANSLATION ﹏﹌

Save for a single entry (more on this below), Kolya's journal was written in Russian.

The scans were used during the translation process.

Because Stanislav's "Eeng-gloosh" was the result of a mere 3-plus years of verbal interaction with his girlfriend Millie, we assigned the main translation to Alton Landau, a former linguistics professor with a keen interest in the languages of the Russian Federation.

Once I was able to sit down and pore through Alton's translation of Kolya's journal, I began to suspect that what we originally received of the PC was not the full document in its entirety.

While I could easily make correlations between entries in either document, there were events Kolya mentions in his journal that, oddly enough, were not commented on at all by Pardo.

I had always suspected that there were gaps in the PC, but I had largely attributed them to Pardo's personal quirks, and his stubborn refusal to document each day, in the standard manner of the average journal.

But now, seeing the content of Kolya's journal, I believe that whoever reached out to us with the scanned PC, furnished us with—ironically enough, given the way we presented portions of the PC in *The Lost Journal*—an *excerpted* copy of the full document.

For whatever reason that person (or persons) may have—whether it was to try and shade Pardo in a light that muted his more disreputable personality traits, or some other reason entirely—we were furnished with an edited version of Pardo's writings.

Or perhaps what we were sent really is all that's left of Pardo's writings.

Perhaps, like all the pages and entries from Kolya's journal that time stole from us, some of Pardo's musings have also been irretrievably lost, and the best we can do is conjecture…

The single entry not written in Russian was in Chavacano, and for that translation, I turned to Hermenegildo Romero, an ex-Jesuit and fellow compound dweller who spent decades in the Philippines before the incident that caused him to leave the Society of Jesus and become a permanent resident here. (He has promised that "one of these fine days," he will share the details of that incident with us.)

Because most of the entries' dates were unfortunately lost due to the journal's damage, we decided to forego dating any of the entries reprinted here.

And while that may keep things in line with Pardo's undated excerpts in the PC, Kolya's journal entries were at least both in chronological order and written on a largely regular basis (both characteristics which Pardo seemed to very pointedly ignore).

While it was tempting to simply reprint all the entries in which Kolya underscored just what an awful and inconsiderate person Pardo actually was, I have instead chosen to reprint particular entries that serve as a kind of "narrative throughline," outlining the general shape of a story whose effects I feel are still being felt today, and not just by Stanislav's family.

Alton's note regarding his translation choices:
It was made clear to me at the beginning of this that the priority was to make the journal comprehensible to a 21st century reader.

Since understandability was more important than preserving the exact tone and voice of the journal writer, I translated the entries in such a way that while some of the 19th century Russian phrasing will still be partially evident, it will also be softened. (Any language from a specific time frame in history will always have its own idiosyncrasies that may seem nonsensical, even alien, to the contemporary reader. Imagine what people a hundred years from now will make of the language of today's youth. Oy!)

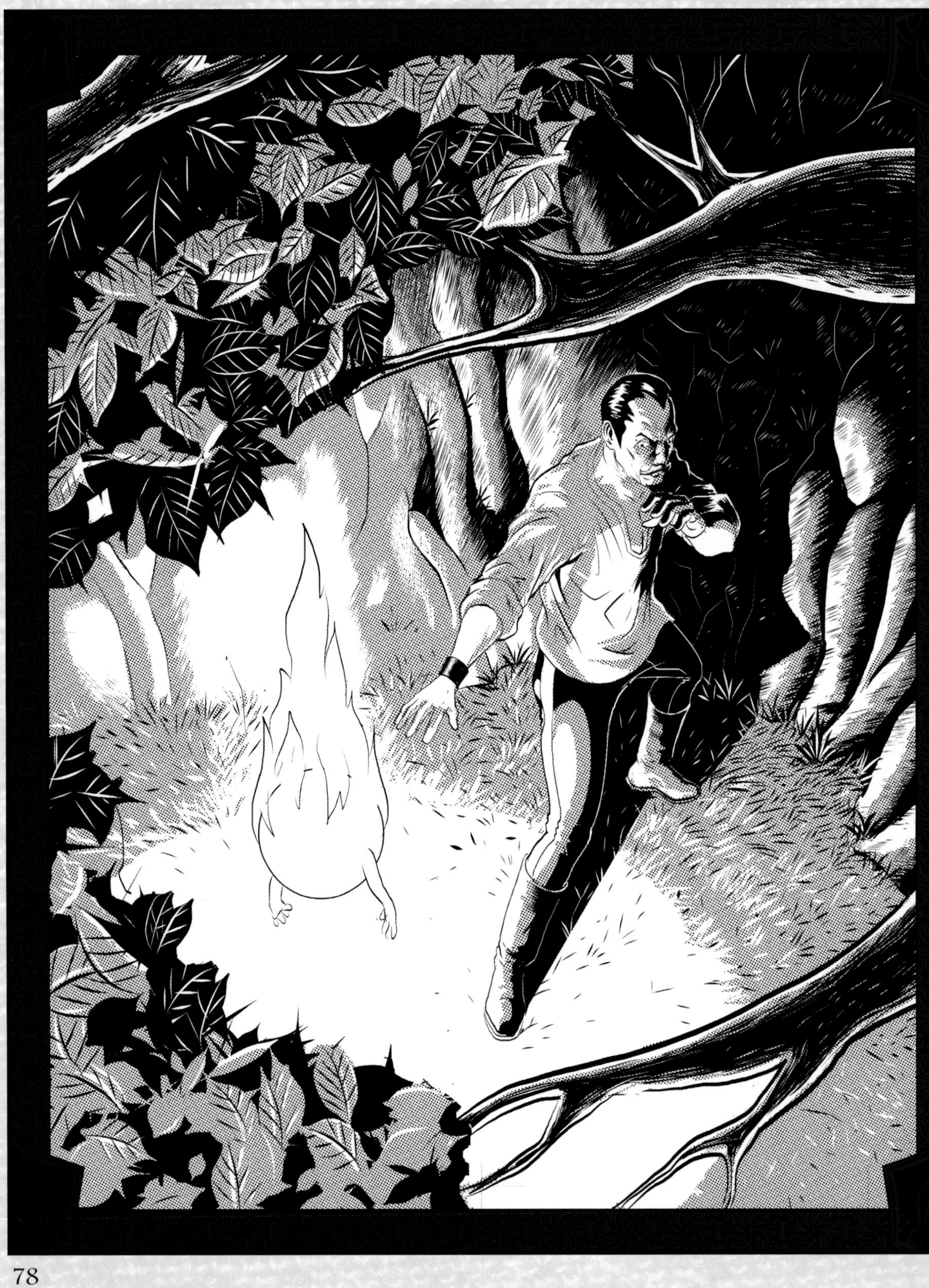

EXCERPTS FROM KOLYA'S JOURNAL
(and conclusions drawn from them)

Kolya the Psychopomp

Alejandro Pardo is a terrible human being.

Which is not to say I am not grateful. I am. Pardo helped my family, and I am unspeakably grateful for that. Which is why I am here, in his oftentimes disagreeable company, in this strange country wrapped in a lush temperate beauty so unlike the cold starkness of home.

I endure his presence because of my family's debt to him.

Yes, he is without a doubt capable and brilliant. And he can be devilishly charming when it suits him.

But that does not make me dislike him any less.

He fights for the rights of his countrymen in one breath, then in the next, derides and ridicules them for their superstition and gullibility.

He is decisive and headstrong, yet apparently feels no responsibility for how his actions impact (sometimes quite disastrously) those who surround him.

He shows no consideration for those he views as beneath him, and given the manner in which he sees himself, only a precious few appear to be the equal of the renowned and esteemed Alejandro Pardo.

I can still hear his goading laughter as he said, "Well, then use the other hand, Kolya!"

Such a terrible human being.

Never mind that plunging my hand into that unearthly ball of flame, with its unsettling feature—the face, forever contorting, as if unable to find even the slightest modicum of rest, those spindly arms, its hands forever grasping yet never actually taking hold of anything—might have cost me my life. If that would be the ultimate cost of Pardo's help in keeping my family safe, then so be it. I would trade that gladly.

The shrewd bastard knows this, of course, which is why he asked me in the first place.

But to ask me to risk my drawing hand…

This is who I am…an artist. So my drawing hand is what defines me, what makes me capable of being my truest self.

And he would have me risk the possibility of that *santelmo* maiming or crippling my hand, all for one of his "experiments"…

Unconscionable.

As soon as my fingers passed into those freezing flames, I knew this simple act was changing me. I didn't know how, not at the time, but I just knew.

And it did.

The nightmares that gripped me the following evening were only the beginning.

But that was also all that I would allow myself to share with Pardo.

I told him about the nightmares, and then left it at that.

Everything that happened afterwards, that will happen from today because of his "experiment," I will not give him the privilege of knowing.

After the nightmares, came the voice.

And I knew this was the dead man's voice.

It was a simple thing that he asked, to pass along a message to his sister, who lived in a small town near the Pardo *hacienda*, which I did as soon as I was able. (I will respect his privacy here and not set down what the message was, though I will say his sister was greatly relieved when I passed it on to her, for she had not even known he had passed away.)

Something that also amazed me was that I found that the memories that had come to me in the nightmares had also left me with a better grasp of the local language.

I am far from being an expert, but I can now converse much better in the vernacular.

Later that evening, I had a dream, and in it, the *santelmo* dimmed, its flames diminishing, its face settling into quietude, until it extinguished completely.

And I knew that the dead man had finally gone on to his eternal rest.

I awoke with a sense of serenity and accomplishment.

I returned to sleep with a smile on my lips.

I thought it would end there, and if it had, perhaps I might have reconsidered my decision and shared this knowledge with Pardo.

But it did not end there.

The following afternoon, even as I was considering the idea of talking to Pardo about my journey to the neighboring town in the role of messenger for the *santelmo*, I heard her. Another voice. And I knew.

Somehow, my act of kindness towards the *santelmo* had become known to other unquiet spirits, and now, this other one was asking for my help.

Again, it was a message, for the family that a lingering, torturous illness had torn her from. They lived nearby as well. So I did for this voice as I had done for the *santelmo*. As soon as I was able, I made the journey (under the pretense of my occasional "excursions," during which I would travel somewhere to sketch and draw whatever caught my eye), and passed along the message.

This time, as soon as her family heard my words, I felt her take leave. I think her family perceived it too, for there was an overwhelming sense of gratitude, and they insisted I stay to partake of a meager meal with them, in a kind of extempore wake.

I do not know whether the woman had become a *santelmo* as well, or whether she was simply an unquiet spirit who could not yet quit this world, but whatever the case, I am glad I could be of assistance to her and her family.

I believe, based on these entries, that the incident where Kolya plunged his hand into the *santelmo* caused him to become a kind of psychopomp, an agent who helped spirits find peace by attending to whatever unfinished business they may have had at the time of their deaths.

As such—and based on everything we know about *santelmo*—the second unquiet spirit Kolya assisted was probably not such a creature, as her family knew she was deceased, since she apparently died after a lengthy illness. *Santelmo* (as mentioned in the LJ) are the spirits of those unfortunate enough to die and not receive a proper burial.

Kolya mentions several other instances of this phenomenon, and a notable aspect here is that, for some of these spirits, there was a woman's voice, belonging to an entity that seemed to be acting as a "mediator," as if those particular spirits could not speak for themselves.

These instances are also notable because what was asked of Kolya was marginally more difficult, more than simply asking him to act as a messenger for the deceased.

Before we return to Kolya's entries, a disclaimer:

Even if my conclusion regarding Kolya becoming a psychopomp is true and makes some kind of logical sense, I am in no way suggesting that anyone who touches a *santelmo* will suddenly become one as well.

I'm of the mind that if that is indeed the case, then Kolya became a psychopomp because he was the exception and not the rule.

I would even go so far as to say that perhaps Kolya was the exception because of the nature of whatever those troubles were back in Russia that Pardo helped him with.

So if anyone out there sees a *santelmo*, touches it, and has their face melt off—a la *Sturmbannführer* Toht, who had the idiot audacity to crack open the Ark of the Covenant—don't say I didn't warn you.

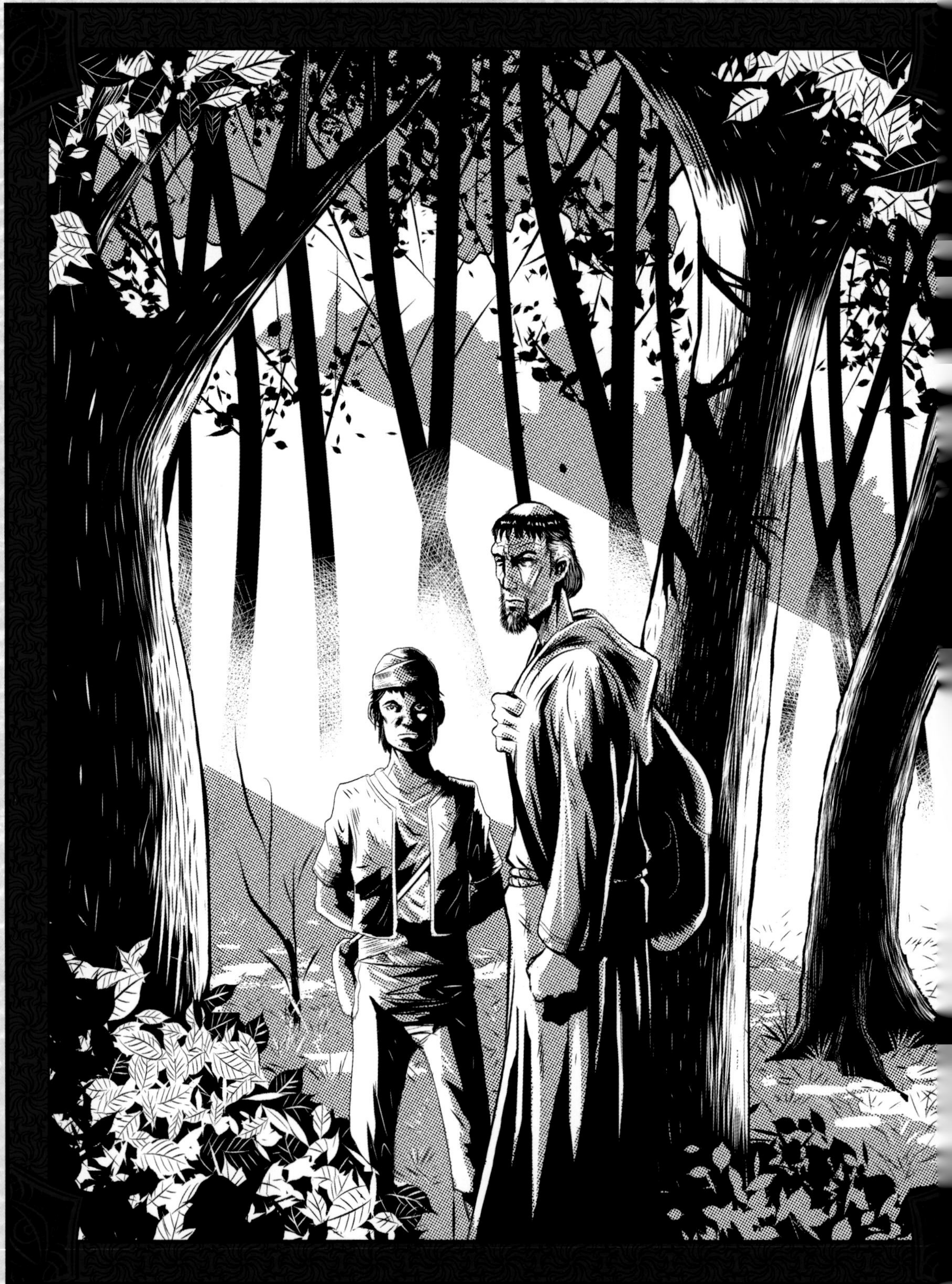

Kolya and the Mutya Experiment

And so others know of my secret now. But better that than allowing Pardo to use me again in one of his "experiments."

Now he wants me to ingest a *mutya*, a kind of mystical jewel. I am to stand under a banana plant's flower at midnight, catch the *mutya* (which shall fall from the flower) in my mouth, and keep it under my tongue as its guardian attempts to wrest it from my possession.

I am told that I need to be brave, and not fear the *mutya*'s keeper, for to fear it means not just the loss of the *mutya*, but my sanity as well.

If I am successful in the struggle for it, then the *mutya* will be mine, and it will make me "the strongest of men," possessed of both an "unfaltering" strength and invulnerability.

But I refuse to be made into a more useful tool by Pardo, to be made into some kind of weapon that he can exploit as he sees fit, as he does with the *tikbalang*.

Which is why I chose to share my secret with Asif and Timoteo.

Thankfully, they are both only too glad to help me.

Timoteo is the *Manggagamot* mentioned in the Pardo journal excerpt in the *Lampong* entry, as well as the Tu-ob section in the LJ. The bastard son of Padre Rubén Abasolo, Timoteo will play a significant role in this section as well as the next.

Just as there appear to be different kinds of *mutya*—some accounts describe a stone, or a pearl, a small ball of flame, or a floating ember—the nature of a *mutya*'s guardian also seems to vary.

Some guardians are said to be *enkanto*, while others are *kapre*, and still others a kind of vicious ogre that goes unnamed, which was also said to have a knack for abducting young women.

As you are about to see, this particular *mutya* seems to have had a guardian of the third variety.

When I shared my misgivings regarding Pardo's motives for asking me to be part of his experiment with the *mutya*, Asif concurred, believing that Pardo wanted someone else in the group to have supernal strength so there would be a force that could, if need be, keep the *tikbalang* at bay.

Asif had also observed that, on occasion, Pardo seems to lose his hold on the *tikbalang*, so much so that there were isolated moments in the past that it appeared the beast was in control, and Pardo was in an impotent rage; that, for those moments, the roles were reversed and the beast was master over him.

As it stands, it seems that, aside from Pardo's control, it is only Marisol who seems able to calm the *tikbalang*.

Asif said that if the *mutya* experiment was a success, he would not be surprised if Pardo would then use me to keep the *tikbalang* in check.

I completely agreed with him.

For his part, Timoteo was relieved that I had chosen to divulge my secret to him, for not only did he feel he could be of assistance in my dealings with the spirits, but he felt that they might also be of assistance in the matter of the *mutya*.

Timoteo seemed particularly interested in my mention of the female voice that sometimes acted as mediator.

He told us he would need to meditate and commune with the multitude of presences that seemed to perennially hover invisibly about him, before he could formulate a sound plan.

In the meantime, he had been able to determine that the particular banana tree that Pardo had been observing would produce the *mutya* on the ninth night after I had decided to take him and Asif into my counsel.

This was enough time for him to meditate and for us all to develop a judicious plan.

We thus went through a series of charades for Pardo, setting up by the banana tree grove before midnight for eight nights in a row, me standing like an idiot beneath its "heart" with my mouth open, waiting for a *mutya* that would not fall.

And once midnight came and went, Asif and I would feign disappointment and watch from the sides of our eyes as Pardo would mask his own dissatisfaction with a display of hearty joviality and a "Well, there's always tomorrow night, gentlemen!"

We did this for eight nights, while Timoteo conceived of a scheme to deal with the *mutya* experiment.

On the morning of the ninth day, Asif and I made a grand show of being utterly disheartened at the nightly disappointments and made tentative suggestions that perhaps, we could take one night off from the *mutya* experiment. Asif would cook up a feast (always good bait to lure Pardo to lower his defenses and more readily see your side of things), we would drink and eat, and perhaps, if we were still capable, traipse over to the grove and give the tree a cursory inspection, just in case.

But Asif and I made it clear: the priority tonight was the feast, and not the experiment.

Pardo was, unsurprisingly, initially resistant to our suggestions, but as the day wore on, and Asif was making another show of contemplating what to prepare for the feast, we could sense Pardo's resistance crumbling, until it finally gave way when Asif settled on preparing *carne de vinha d'alhos* (a Portuguese variation of adobo which includes wine in its sauce) and torta de *huevo*, stuffed to bursting with cheese and chorizo.

The moment Pardo took that first taste of the *carne de vinha d'alhos* and the smile spread wide on his lips, we knew the initial part of the plan was going to succeed.

Being the cook for the evening, it was ridiculously easy for Asif to ensure that Pardo's food was laced with a powder that included in its composition, traces of the local *talampunay*, the thorn apple, or as the Spaniards call it, toloache.

The *talampunay* can be poisonous, and if I did not trust in Asif's skill as an assassin (for he has, after all, been trained in this discipline since he was a child), and his certitude that the dose Pardo would ingest would not be a fatal one, I might have asked that we forego that aspect of the plan.

But Asif was true to his word: Pardo's drugged food, coupled with the copious amount of wine he imbibed, gradually sent him into a drunken stupor. Meanwhile, Asif, Timoteo (whom we had Pardo invite to the feast, along with Timoteo's father, Padre Rubén), and I had to indulge in another charade, as we feigned drunkenness in measured step with Pardo's own, very real, inebriation.

For a few moments, I was actually concerned that Pardo would see through Timoteo's pitiful approximation of a drunken state, for he was not quite as *loud* as he tends to be when inebriated.

Thankfully, Pardo was himself too drunk and groggy to notice.

All this transpired well before midnight, but we still made a show of it for Marisol. That we, the drunken three, Asif, Timoteo, and I, would stagger and stumble over to the grove just to be certain that the *mutya* experiment was still tended to, despite Pardo's deeply satisfied slumber.

So we left Marisol to tend to Pardo (and the *tikbalang*, for Asif had noticed that Pardo's control over the beast would often slip when he was drunk and not in full control of his own faculties).

Padre Rubén, having noted his son's odd drunkenness, accompanied us as well, but only after a sworn oath that what he would witness was to be kept secret from both Pardo and Marisol.

Padre Rubén, ever the rascal, agreed instantly.

So we went, three of us acting like drunken buffoons as loudly as we could for the first few minutes, so that Marisol could hear us, but dropping the pretense as soon as we were reasonably out of her ear-shot.

And as we walked towards the grove, Timoteo recounted to his father a short recollection of the events that had brought us here this summer night, the full moon above us.

Thus did we arrive at the grove, and while the other three waited nearby, I walked to the banana tree, its blossom facing the east, ready to expel its treasure.

I think we all waited with bated breath, until finally, there it was, the *mutya*, catching the moonlight as it slipped past the "heart's" opening lips.

The *mutya* fell, and I caught it easily in my mouth, and it felt warm, and alive, as I quickly slid it beneath my tongue.

In the distance, I heard Padre Rubén's sudden intake of breath, and I knew that the guardian had arrived. I turned to look, and there it was, a brutish ogre, so very tall, and black, and hairy, and <u>naked</u>, running through the banana trees towards me.

And I <u>laughed</u>.

I laughed because the brute's manhood swung to and fro in a most vigorous and aggressive manner, as if it possessed an anger all its own, as if it might, of its own accord, batter and bludgeon me into submission.

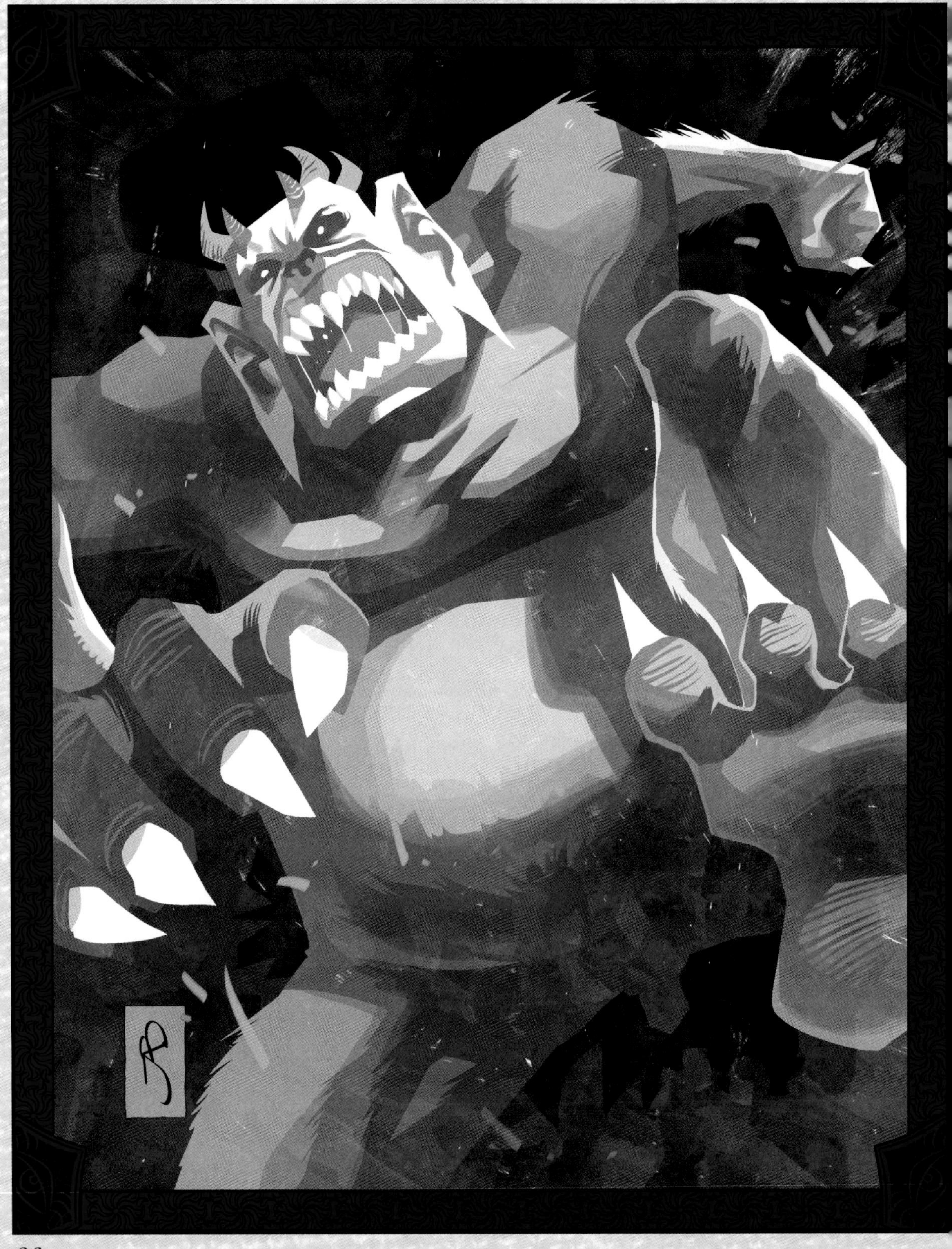

Now, as an artist, I am not a stranger to the naked form of either sex, and look upon it in an aesthetic sense and not a lewd one. Even in that tiny sliver of a moment, I could see that the fiend had a feral majesty all its own, as does a lion or a bear. My eyes immediately established that its size and proportions were rather pleasing, and I would not have balked if I had been asked to draw the creature's likeness.

It was not out of prurience or even mockery that I laughed. It was simply because the sight of it seemed so <u>ridiculous</u> given the circumstances.

I also believe that laugh was a release of the tension I felt in that moment: keeping yet another secret from Pardo, a man who had saved my family and yet I occasionally loathed, and who we had drugged (more to the point, <u>poisoned</u>) just an hour or so ago.

And I was now about to face a raging ogre in a struggle that, should I fail, would cost my sanity. It was all so <u>ludicrous</u>.

And so I laughed.

More like a short, sharp bark, really, given that I was concerned I might spit out the *mutya* if I laughed any more. But that single sound was most definitely a laugh.

At first, Timoteo and the others thought that I had somehow already gone mad, but the *Manggagamot* saw the same thing I did.

The brute stumbled, flinching at the sound I made. It paused, and stared at me, as if uncertain how it might react. Then it spared a quick glance to its manhood—for it knew, instinctively, that it was at the sight of this that I had laughed—before it looked back at me with a newfound ferocity on its features.

It roared, and resumed its charge, but the damage had already been done.

Timoteo saw the same thing I did, and he knew <u>exactly</u> how to exploit it.

He told his father and Asif to laugh, to laugh as loud and as boisterously as they were able, and my dear friends did precisely that.

They laughed, the three of them, for I could not, and even as the ogre raged towards me, I could see the laughter piercing its pride as if they were arrows and spears.

It was still terribly strong, of course, and when it rammed into me, it was all I could do to not have all the breath smashed out of me, and to keep my mouth firmly shut.

We wrestled, the guardian and I, as it tried to choke me. It smelled of unwashed flesh and desperation, its eyes blazing with an anger that was fueled by the shame that my compatriots' laughter elicited from it.

But somehow I knew, the fight had already fled from it; the moment I had barked out that single, sharp laugh, I had already won.

Timoteo had spoken of some men who had struggled with a *mutya*'s guardian for <u>hours</u>, but this one did not even last half of an hour.

As we wrestled on the ground, and my friends assailed it with their laughter, its strength and purpose seemed to ebb, until finally, I forced its hands off me, and it retaliated by simply pushing me roughly away.

It stood, and I could see disgust and self-loathing in its frame, and the laughter stopped, cut off abruptly.

The brute took a final, reproachful look at me, darted a quick glance to its manhood, then walked silently away, its shoulders slumped in shameful defeat.

It was only when the ogre had disappeared back into the night that I again heard my friends as they rushed towards me in jubilant celebration.

I was mildly surprised to find that I was still sprawled out on the ground, which I only belatedly realized when a widely grinning Asif held out his hand to help me to my feet.

I then proceeded to the next phase of Timoteo's plan: I took the vial that the *Manggagamot* had prepared and carefully expelled the *mutya* into its open mouth, while Timoteo whispered feverishly beneath his breath.

He took the vial and quickly capped it, and even as I watched, the *mutya* softened, liquefied into some kind of dew, and then all Timoteo seemed to hold in his hand was a vial of liquid that sparkled intermittently in the moonlight.

This bit of sorcery was achieved with the help of the spirits. Because they knew that I would be of assistance to some of their kind, they agreed to Timoteo's request to preserve the *mutya*, so that while I would not use it, its innate power would still be contained within it, while also making it undetectable to creatures like its guardian, for a *mutya* was not meant to be left lying around, unused. Its power would emanate from it as the delectable aroma of Asif's cooking would from a half-lidded dish, and if not for the spirits' spells, the *mutya* would be a magnet for all sorts of unnatural trouble.

The spirits told Timoteo that the *mutya* was now quiescent, but could be awakened when the time and the "right scion" held it in his hand. I take this to mean that sometime, the *mutya* will come into use, to help my family. Perhaps it will be my son, or perhaps some distant descendant in some far off time, but someone will take it, and swallow it, and become what I could be right now, but choose not to, because I know that if I do, Pardo will only use and misuse me for his own gain.

Asif once said something that has always haunted me: He said that it astounded him how Pardo could not even see that what he had done to the *tikbalang* was precisely the same thing that the Spaniards had done to his countrymen. That he was, in essence and in deed, exactly the same as those he so despised.

Asif observed: "For someone who is so clearly very brilliant, Pardo can be so stupid about the simplest of things."

Another message the spirits shared with Timoteo was that one day, someone from my family would help them with a "monumental labor," and that they hoped that person would be just as noble and valiant and true as I. I asked Timoteo if this "someone" was also the "right scion," and he replied that he wasn't certain, but he didn't think so.

As I took the vial that contained the *mutya* from Timoteo, I thanked the spirits beneath my breath, hoping they understood, and could see the depths of my gratitude.

We walked back to Pardo's *hacienda* then, and on our journey, I felt a stab of guilt, at my unintended ridicule of the ogre, but then I quickly realized that it was that same manhood that I had not meant to deride that the brute undoubtedly used to terrorize the women these contemptible beasts were fond of abducting.

And upon realizing that, I could only hope that tonight's events had distressed and shamed the fiend enough that it would never do so again.

Hours later, when we were all finally roused from our slumbers rather late in the day, and after seeing Padre Rubén and Timoteo off (they returned to the nearby *barangay* with a heavy load of the extra food Asif always prepared whenever he cooked for Pardo, so the local townsfolk could also partake of the feast), Asif and I played raconteur and told a very tall tale of having arrived at the grove a bit too late, some anonymous fool already swallowing the *mutya* as we watched agape.

We pantomimed like idiots, as we told our agreed-upon fiction, keeping Pardo entertained with the story of the anonymous fool wrestling with the *mutya*'s foul guardian, and how he lost the struggle and went quite mad, running off into the night, babbling and yowling. This last bit was accompanied by a side-splitting performance by Asif of some drooling imbecile that made Pardo laugh so hard he complained anew of his pounding headache.

Meanwhile, I have secreted the vial where no one—least of all, Pardo—may find it.

I hope some new "experiment" captures his fancy, so the matter of the *mutya* will be summarily expelled from his thoughts.

As is plainly evident, Stanislav is the "right scion" the spirits spoke of, though what characteristics or traits made him "right" are unclear.

Perhaps Stanislav was fated to be the "right scion," or perhaps what happened to him would have happened eventually with one of Kolya's descendants, and circumstance merely laid it upon his shoulders.

As to the "monumental labor" also mentioned by the spirits, I believe this was part of the price the spirits asked in return for their help with the *mutya*.

I also believe I know the event this phrase referred to: what is known as the "Petrozavodsk phenomenon" or the "Petrozavodsk incident," which took place on September 20, 1977.

Sadly, a key individual who may be able to shed considerable light on my theory is hesitant to go on record.

I completely understand the hesitation and choose not to push.

If the interview eventually does take place, then perhaps we will be able to delve into the "monumental labor," and how I believe that ties in to both the Petrozavodsk phenomenon, and the circumstances of how Kolya's journal came to be in the possession of Stanislav's uncle Yefim.

As a quick (and deeply gratifying) footnote to the *mutya*'s guardian, it is telling—given the manner in which Kolya and his compatriots were able to overcome it—that it is believed that the way an abducted woman may escape captivity is by striking its "manhood."

So, remember, ladies: If you see a brutish ogre running straight for you, keep your eyes trained on his "manhood" and give it a good. Solid. KICK!

And you don't even need a *mutya* to do that.

Kolya's subsequent entries seem to indicate a return to normalcy for the group ("normalcy" being a very relative term here, of course), and Pardo becomes absorbed with other concerns, so there is no further talk about the "failure" of the *mutya* experiment.

Kolya, likewise, does not mention it further, though he continues to help unquiet spirits whenever he is asked.

The following section features entries that recount an incident whose full ramifications I believe we have yet to experience.

Alejandro Pardo and the Crocodile with the Black Tongue

It is hard for me to imagine that not even a full day has passed since Pardo told us about his meeting.

I thought this would be easy.

I suppose I should have known better.

Asif and I were having a late breakfast when Pardo entered the kitchen and told us of his plans for the evening, plans that he had already apparently volunteered us for.

He was to meet someone shortly before midnight at a nearby river, someone who was eager to form an alliance with Pardo against the Spaniards. There was some talk of rebellion and revolution, and Pardo seemed eager for his clandestine appointment.

We were to lie in wait and observe, and support him, should there be any trouble.

Pardo was still cautious, after all, despite his obvious eagerness, for this was to be his first face-to-face meeting with his prospective conspirator.

Asif and I readily agreed, for we too could see that the Spaniards' colonization of these islandswas a terrible injustice. It was an added inducement that this particular excursion did not involveanything out of the ordinary.

Or so we thought.

Asif agreed with Pardo's plan to journey to the appointed meeting place (a bridge over a nearby river) separately.

But when Asif and I arrived at the spot that had been agreed would be our vantage point, the distance to the bridge, as well as the intervening terrain, proved to be cause for worry. If something went awry, we could not possibly get to Pardo's side in time to be of any help.

This situation was complicated even more because we did not have the use of a spyglass. We had lost our field-glass during the *ikugan* encounter, and Pardo had yet to receive delivery of another.

We could still see the bridge of course, though the distance and the dark compromised our vision substantially.

Asif and I had no time for discussion, though. We had only just arrived at the vantage point, when we spotted Pardo at one end of the bridge, and another figure—robed and hooded—across the river, at the other.

We watched as the distant figures walked slowly out onto the bridge. Being a rickety thing, merely planks of weathered wood and gradually fraying rope, it was the kind of bridge I would not trust my weight to, and yet both Pardo and the robed figure stepped out onto it, and proceeded to slowly walk towards its middle.

The whole encounter appeared precarious, as the section of the river directly below the bridge was known to be infested with crocodiles.

I thought I heard, once or twice, the labored creaking of the bridge well over the sound of the rushing river waters, though that is quite possibly my imagination having gotten the better of me.

Pardo and the robed figure met at the bridge's middle, and they seemed to stand there on that swaying bridge for what felt like an eternity.

Then it happened, and Asif and I were running down towards the bridge like lunatics at full moon.

All the while we ran, I was not even certain who fell off the bridge.

One moment, they were there, at its middle—and though they were certainly having a discussion, distance and the sound of the river precluded any possibility of eavesdropping; the next, there was a sudden and very quick flurry. One had hit the other, who then toppled off the bridge and into the river.

Asif and I did not even spare a single moment to see who had struck the blow and remained on the swaying bridge, and who had fallen into the water, without a doubt now a surprise for the crocodiles.

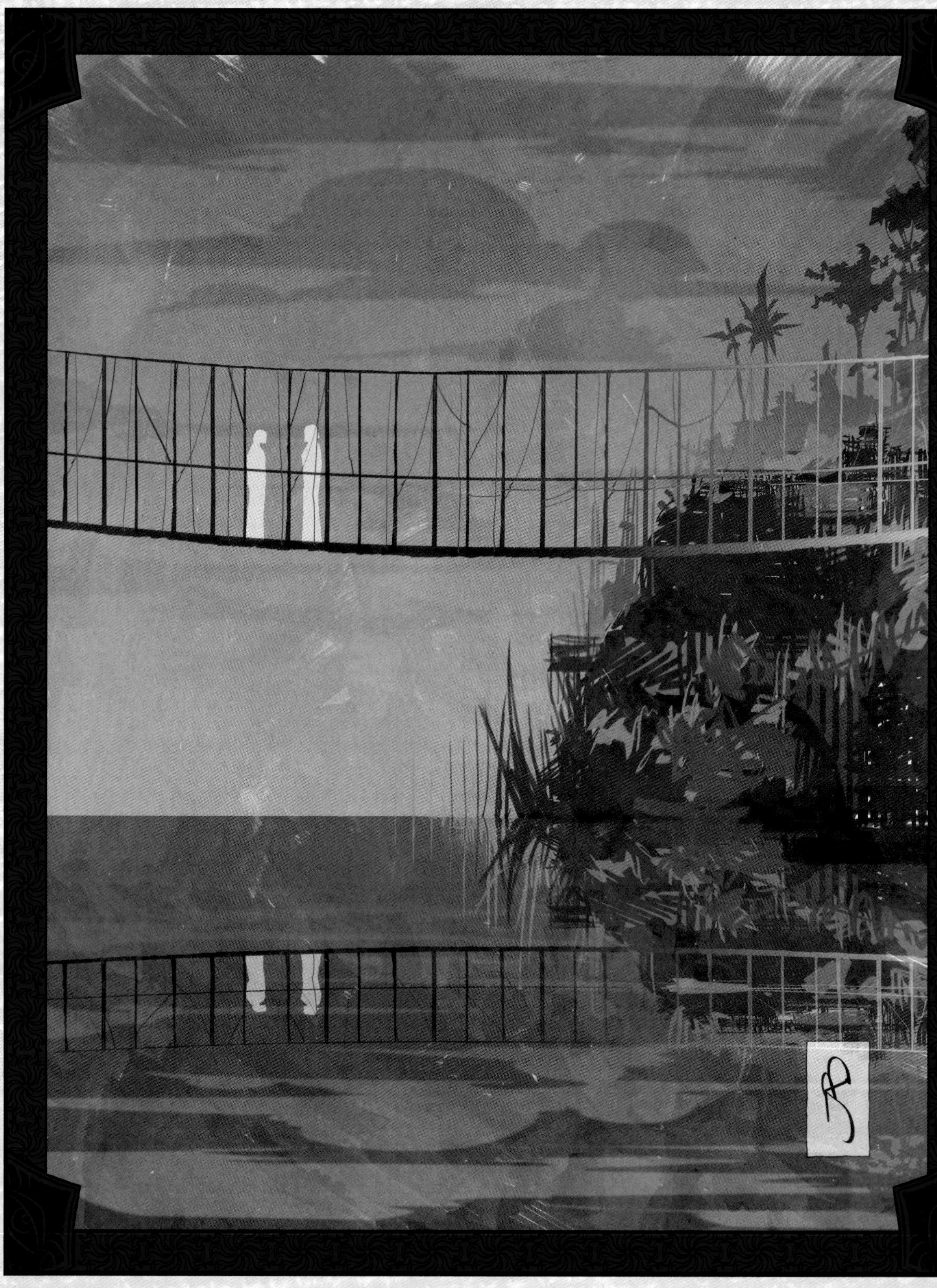

Even before we reached the bridge, however, we knew who was who: Pardo was the one still standing, for we could hear his tempestuous swearing long before we reached his side.

"Did you see? Did you see?!" he demanded angrily.

"No, not really," Asif replied, and though he knew better than to look out towards the river, I did. I looked, even though I already knew, just as Asif did.

I'd seen the crocodiles go about their work before.

If the robed figure wasn't on either bank—and I could see no sign of any other than the three of us—then there was no hope he (or she) would ever surface.

"What happened?" I asked. Or perhaps it was Asif who asked—I'm not entirely sure anymore. Pardo's reply was curt. "Not here."

And so the three of us slunk off like thieves in the night.

Pardo related to us what had taken place on the bridge on our journey back to the *hacienda*:

The robed figure (a woman, Pardo noted, judging by her "alluring" voice) was indeed the person he was supposed to meet; from opposite sides of the bridge, the correct passwords were exchanged.

They walked towards each other, and then spoke when they met at the bridge's middle.

The discussion was proceeding apace, and Pardo said they had what appeared to be a vast area of common ground upon which to build their proposed alliance against the Spaniards.

Despite the tantalizing suggestion of fellowship, and her undeniable comeliness (which Pardo claimed she exuded "as if she were naked and not bundled up in those unseemly burlap robes"), he began to suspect that the woman was not exactly what she appeared to be.

Their conversation began to turn contentious, until finally, the woman admitted the truth, and in what Pardo described as "a fit of revulsion and rage at being made a fool of by her conniving duplicity," he struck her on the temple, and stunned, she tumbled off the bridge.

"She said she was a *BOROKA*."

"And what is that?" I asked, for that was the first time I had heard the word.

"It's what the Iloko call a *Manananggal*."

I was speechless, and from his silence, I imagine Asif was as well.

"You see why I had to do it, don't you?" And there was a strange kind of pleading in the way Pardo asked the question, as if he desperately needed us to concur with him.

"Did she threaten you in any way?" Asif asked.

And I could see this had been the wrong question to pose, for Pardo bristled upon hearing it.

"She was a *Manananggal*, Asif. Would you care to imagine how many poor souls she's left as nothing more than sacks of skin and bone, oozing the most noisome fluids?! Not to mention how many women she's violated in her lifetime?! How many lives-yet-to-be she's extinguished?!"

"I wouldn't have to imagine if she were here to ask, now would I?" was Asif's rapier reply.

"She wasn't human, Asif."

I looked at Pardo then, and I could see his eyes blazing with some kind of disquieting fervor.

"She was dangerous."

Before we proceed with Kolya's entries, I would like to take this opportunity to point out that nowhere in the PC does Pardo mention this incident on the bridge.

Which could mean one of three things:

A) Kolya invented the entire scenario for his journal, which somehow, I doubt.

B) My theory that we were provided with an excerpted version of Pardo's writings is true.

C) This is telling evidence of the guilt Pardo experienced because of the incident, inasmuch as the obstinate, opinionated, and hubristic larger-than-life persona that was Alejandro Pardo could feel so mundane an emotion as guilt.

If C is true, then he was so guilt-ridden that he consciously chose to omit the entire incident from his quasi-memoir.

And even if C is true, that still does not exclude the possibility of B.

On the matter of the *BOROKA:*

While it is true that "*BOROKA*" is the Ilokano term for a *Manananggal*, there are reports (unconfirmed to date) where, unlike the *Manananggal* as described in the LJ, a *BOROKA* is characterized alternately as:

A) A "self-segmenter" like a *Manananggal*, but whose wings are feathered, like an avian's;

B) Retaining a human head and torso, yet having the four legs of a horse and avian wings.

I have diffculty picturing the anatomical feasibility of the Type B *BOROKA* (how do we connect four equine legs to a human torso?).

Unless, of course, these accounts fail to mention that the Type B also has the barrel of a horse, in which case, it would more readily resemble a winged centaur.

The Type A *BOROKA*, meanwhile, appears to have a specific liking for human hearts and livers, which she gouges out of her victims with her sharp claws. No long, tubular tongue and organ-liquefying (see *Manananggal* entry in LJ).

Which leads me to the conclusion that, despite the Ilocanos' interchangeability of the terms, a *BOROKA* is possibly a different species from (whether it's either of the two Types), or perhaps an evolutionary offshoot of, the *Manananggal* (if it's Type A).

Additionally, while the Type A has been said to be a child-eater, there are also claims that she abducts boys so they can be her housekeeper.

That is disturbing on so many levels, I don't even know where to start…

We must also note from Pardo's heated words to Asif, that at the time of the incident, he seems to believe that the *Boroka* is identical to the *Manananggal*.

It is, once more, telling that Pardo makes no substantial mention of the *Boroka* in the PC, not just the *BOROKA* on the bridge, but any *Boroka* in general.

It's possible that this was the only encounter the group had with one.

And it appears to have been one that was offering the prospect of an alliance to form some kind of proactive rebellion against the Spaniards more than half a century before the formation of the Katipunan.

Once again, I shake my head at the folly of Alejandro Pardo.

A final note regarding the *BOROKA:*

I find it intriguing that, like the *enkanto*, the term used to identify the *Boroka* is a word that is rooted in the Spanish language. ("*Encanto*" means "charm," "glamor," or "spell.")

"*Boroka*" stems from "*bruja*," which means "witch" or "night-hag."

Does the term's etymology have a deeper significance beyond linguistics, in the same way that Pardo theorized the *enkanto* are not actually native to the Philippines?

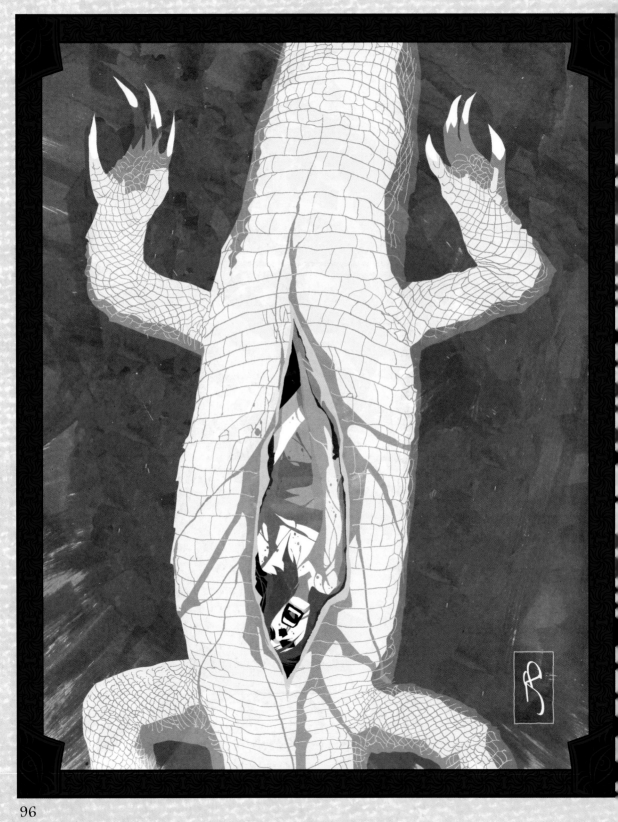

After I penned yesterday's entry, I desperately wanted the succor of sleep, but it evaded me with what felt like a fair amount of scorn.

So it was that even before the sun had risen, I was already leaving the *hacienda*, on my way to pay Padre Rubén and Timoteo a visit.

It was quite possibly this early departure that prevented me from witnessing the incident that occurred at the river bank.

Asif himself only arrived at the site as the incident was coming to its close.

From conversations we conducted with the eyewitnesses, this was what we could piece together:

Shortly before dawn, a crocodile was found on the river bank.

While the beast appeared dead, it was noted (to the dread of many of the townsfolk) that its tongue was grossly swollen and black.

Several individuals then claim to have heard a voice issue from within the crocodile. Alarmed that perhaps there was a victim still alive inside it, the beast's belly was slit open.

While there was indeed a body found whole and intact in the crocodile's stomach, the body (none of the townsfolk we spoke to seemed certain whether it was man or woman) appeared to be dead as well.

It was at this point that Asif came upon the commotion on the river bank.

Asif had journeyed to the town for much the same reason I had made my way to Timoteo and his father: to help clear the clutter of thoughts left in the wake of last night's events at the bridge.

Asif had intended to purchase some herbs, for cooking always served to calm him, but the hubbub led him to the river bank.

Quickly navigating the agitated crowd, Asif reached the crocodile's side just as its belly was slit open.

Asif saw the unmoving body, and he was certain it was female, for she was naked, and pulled into herself, like an infant asleep in its mother's womb.

Even as the townsfolk nearest stepped away from the gruesome sight, Asif is certain that in that moment, the woman opened her eyes and glared balefully at him.

There was then a noxious reek, as the crocodile's corpse emitted a cloud of smoke, and this drove the townsfolk back even more, though Asif stood his ground, forearm to his nose, tensed and ready for some dire eventuality.

When the smoke cleared, leaving only the faintest traces of the fetor, the corpse of the crocodile with the black tongue, as well as the loathsome bounty it carried in its stomach, was gone.

There was an imprint of its bulk on the damp soil of the river bank, but the corpse itself had, impossibly, vanished along with the smoke (or perhaps, had become the smoke).

In the interim, after I had shared the events of last night with Timoteo and Padre Rubén (who had emitted a censorious "Tut!" when he heard what Pardo had done), I once again asked for their utmost confidence, and then proceeded to prepare for my journey back to the *hacienda*.

Padre Rubén suggested that Timoteo accompany me on the trek, and I knew this was because he was concerned for my state of mind, but could not himself be available for he had his parish duties to attend to.

So Timoteo and I headed back to the *hacienda*, and it was on our way there that we came across a small group of townsfolk who seemed both agitated and excited.

There was a confused chorus of replies when we asked what the matter was, and all we could be certain of was that whatever had caused them to be in such a state, it had taken place on the river bank.

One of them also mentioned they had spotted Asif there, so Timoteo and I quickly bid them farewell, and hastened to the river.

We arrived to find the townsfolk in a superstitious uproar, and while I had no trouble finding Asif (he was still rooted to the spot, staring down at the impression of the now-vanished crocodile on the ground), Timoteo was all but mobbed by the anxious crowd, for his reputation as a *Manggagamot* was well-known and appreciated by many.

Timoteo did his best to calm them, while also getting as clear a picture as he could of the events as they had transpired. Surrounded by the distressed crowd, he gradually made his way to us, and to the spot on the river bank where the crocodile's corpse had been found.

All of the townsfolk who had been dogging his steps now stopped well clear of the spot, leaving Timoteo to make the rest of way towards us.

We could hear the townsfolk mutter and conjecture amongst themselves.

Timoteo seemed to block all of that out and fell into some kind of waking trance as he crouched down by the depression in the damp soil.

Minutes that seemed like hours passed, as Timoteo whispered feverishly beneath his breath.

Then he stood up, and turned to address the townsfolk.

He told them something "dark and wicked" had been among them, but was gone now. He told them he would cleanse this spot, and then lay down charms and wards to protect them, should the "beast" return. He told them he would pray to the *Buwaya* for guidance, and that they would surely not forsake his pleas, for the crocodile was their child, and they would certainly have something to say on the matter.

This seemed to quell the anxiety of the crowd, and they began to drift off to resume the routine that had been so ferociously disrupted by the events of the morning.

Timoteo was pale and shaken as he turned to us to say he did indeed need to commune with the spirits and to pray to the *Buwaya*, for what had transpired here was no trifling matter.

Timoteo took his leave, and Asif and I stayed and spoke to the eyewitnesses.

Afterwards, unwilling yet to return to the *hacienda*, Asif and I decided to see if we could be of any assistance to Timoteo.

When we arrived at the church, Padre Rubén said Timoteo was at the spring, which meant that he was praying to the *Buwaya*, and in those matters, Asif and I were of absolutely no use.

So we made ourselves useful to Padre Rubén, and helped in any way we could to ease his parish duties (which was the excuse we gave to Pardo at day's end, once we returned to the *hacienda*).

Two things:

One — Again, there is absolutely no mention of the incident at the river bank in the PC. I find it highly improbable that Pardo would not have heard of it, given how quickly news can spread in a small community and its nearby territories. The startling, supranatural aspect of the event would have made it a prime candidate as fodder for this kind of hearsay.

And if I properly grasp the geography of the area in which Pardo's *hacienda* is located—gleaned from the entries, for we have yet to properly pinpoint the *hacienda's* actual location, because of the frustrating lack of place names— then the river bank in question is the same one where Pardo had his *Buwaya* sighting (see *Buwaya* entry in the LJ); again, just one more reason why it seems odd that he makes no mention of another out-of-the-ordinary incident in the same spot.

Two — This is the background of the "spring" Kolya mentions in his entry, as pieced together by me, from several entries in both the PC and Kolya's journal.

On the day of Timoteo's birth, as Padre Rubén hurried towards the house of his expectant lover (a local widow who had lost her husband while she was still in her early 20's), he passed a spot on the edges of the parish grounds, and there was a single, very large paw print, of what had surely been a *Buwaya*, and not a mere crocodile.

Harried as he was to be by his lover's side, all Padre Rubén did was to take quick note of the paw print (which he saw was filled with water that sparkled in the sunlight) without stopping.

At the end of a long, hectic day, and with the sight of his healthy newborn son still firmly entrenched in his mind, Padre Rubén returned the way he had come, to find that where he had seen the paw print earlier, there was now a fair-sized spring.

This time, Padre Rubén stopped, awed by the sight of this body of water that was not there mere hours earlier. Padre Rubén believed that the water that he had seen in the paw print had continued to flow, upwards, from some vast miraculous reservoir, and that this was a sign from the *Buwaya*, a blessing, for his newborn Timoteo.

> And when Timoteo came of age, and when it was clear that his path was that of the *Manggagamot*, the young man chose to build his home by the spring, whose waters were said to be always clear and pure, and even during times of drought, retained its water levels, as if its source could never be depleted.
>
> And because it seemed that Padre Rubén's belief regarding the origins of the spring was true, whenever Timoteo needed to pray and make offerings to the *Buwaya*, he would do so at the spring, instead of the river banks, where the townsfolk would normally pay their obeisance.

When Timoteo returned, he seemed both exhausted and focused on what it was he needed to do.

He told us that he needed to communicate with the "beast," because the *Buwaya* needed to know its intentions. He said that while he would initiate the dialogue, someone else was needed to act as the channel through which it would communicate.

And the best candidate for that, according to the *Buwaya*, was me.

My rational mind understood, of course. If this "beast" was no longer living exactly, then perhaps it was something like an unquiet spirit, and I had experience with unquiet spirits, so yes, I was the best candidate.

But that did not stop me from feeling a deep well of anxiety bubble up within me.

Timoteo and I prepared for the coming ordeal together.

Padre Rubén was our accomplice in this matter, telling Pardo that he would be in need of my services at the parish for "half of a week, perhaps more," for there was much physical labor in need of doing.

I stayed in Timoteo's home, and we fasted and prepared ourselves, spending many an hour by the spring in silence.

It is the night of the new moon, and we have gathered in the large storage room of the church: Padre Rubén, Asif, and of course, Timoteo and myself.

The *Manggagamot* has laid down the wards for our protection, and Padre Rubén added his own blessings.

Timoteo says he has also cast wards in my mind and my soul, so that the "beast" will not have access to my thoughts nor my emotions.

I am sat before the table, upon which my journal—this journal—is laid open.

I am mildly disturbed that in a few moments, I will still be writing in these pages, but it will not really be me. It will not be my mind controlling the actions of my hand.

Timoteo says this is the best way to allow for communication. If he lets the "beast" speak through me, there is no telling what damage may be done to my larynx.

Following is the single Chavacano entry in Kolya's journal, translated into English by Hermenegildo Romero.

Hermenegildo's note regarding the entry:

It was frankly disturbing to see that single entry in another handwriting entirely, as if written by some other person.

The handwriting was both softer, more feminine, and far more vehement and ferocious. Even in the scanned reproduction, the pressure on the paper was obvious. The page on which the entry was written was practically torn by the force with which these words were set down. And that's not even taking into account the terrible condition of the journal itself...

The entry is written in the Ermiteño dialect. According to John Holm's Pidgins and Creoles, there were reportedly some 15,000 speakers of this dialect in Ermita, as of 1942.

Sadly, we flash forward over seven decades later, and Ermiteño is now considered an extinct language.

Given the extent of my (admittedly-not-expert-levels of) knowledge, I have no idea how rare a written sample of Ermiteño is.

If not for the entry's brevity and disturbing content, this might have been regarded as an important linguistic record.

I pray no damage is done to my hand.
My safety now lies completely in the hands of my friends.
I hope to pen many more entries once this night is over.

No! You will not speak and ask me questions!
I shall not be your puppet!
I shall tell you what you wish to know, but I shall do the telling!

You have warded this one. I cannot see into him, and I cannot see what he fears, what he desires.
You think you are smart...
Your friend did this to me!

No… not your friend…
I can smell your reaction to the word…
He is not your friend, then.
He is your master. Or believes himself to be your master.
And he will be your death, as he was mine!

I wanted the same thing he did! For these invaders to leave these shores!
I had hopes we could form an alliance. Foolish hopes, I see now.
I was warned of him. I was told he would not listen and that I was stupid for believing he would see reason.
I see they were right to warn me.
He is like the worst kind of child, only want and need, without thought for anyone else. He is a blight, that one. He will do what is in his nature, blind to the damage he wreaks upon those around him.

I offered my hand, a temporary truce, until we drove the usurpers from these islands! But he could not see past his suspicion! Such a narrow, little mind…

I shall sleep now. Sleep long and dream.

Part of me was witch, another part crocodile.
Now I am both and neither.

I was the Severed. I was the Black Tongue That Could Not Move.
Now I am both and neither.

I was alive, then I was dead.
Now I am both and neither.

And when I awaken, I shall be something beautiful.

And new.

And terrible.

Kolya's next entry is dated a week later.

I am still convalescing and have spent most of the past week trying to write properly again.

This is the first time I am satisfied that my penmanship appears as it normally should, though my hand still tires and cramps more quickly than usual.

> The entries that follow are each gradually longer than the previous one, as Kolya appears to continue to recover (though I feel I must point out that the quality of his penmanship never really does return to its former state). What follows is a summary of those entries.

Pardo was apparently told that during Kolya's stay at the parish, he contracted "breakbone fever" (dengue), and was advised to extend his stay with Padre Rubén and Timoteo to recover.

Kolya's recovery involved much bed rest as well as being plied with herbal concoctions prepared by Timoteo; among these was an ointment that was rubbed on Kolya's arm, particularly on his forearm, wrist, and hand.

Timoteo also said that the healing was helped along tremendously by the spirits who were pleased with Kolya's assistance and kindness towards the unquiet of their kind.

During one of Asif's visits to Kolya, Asif recounted how, on that night of the new moon, just before the frenzied writing in the journal began, there was a moment when Kolya looked straight at him, and it was that same "baleful glare" that the naked woman in the crocodile's stomach had given him on the river bank, as if her eyes had replaced Kolya's.

Timoteo communed with the *Buwaya*, in what seems to have been some kind of debriefing, as he related the events of the night of the new moon, and what had been written in the journal.

Timoteo was told that the "sleep" that the Beast mentioned would last a long time, "by the count of your kind and of our children." That it "would awaken long after you and yours have been allowed to ride upon our backs."

But the *Buwaya* assured Timoteo they would help to prepare for the Beast's awakening.

Before we get to that, though, yes, I have chosen, for lack of a better name, to take a cue from Timoteo and call it "the Beast."

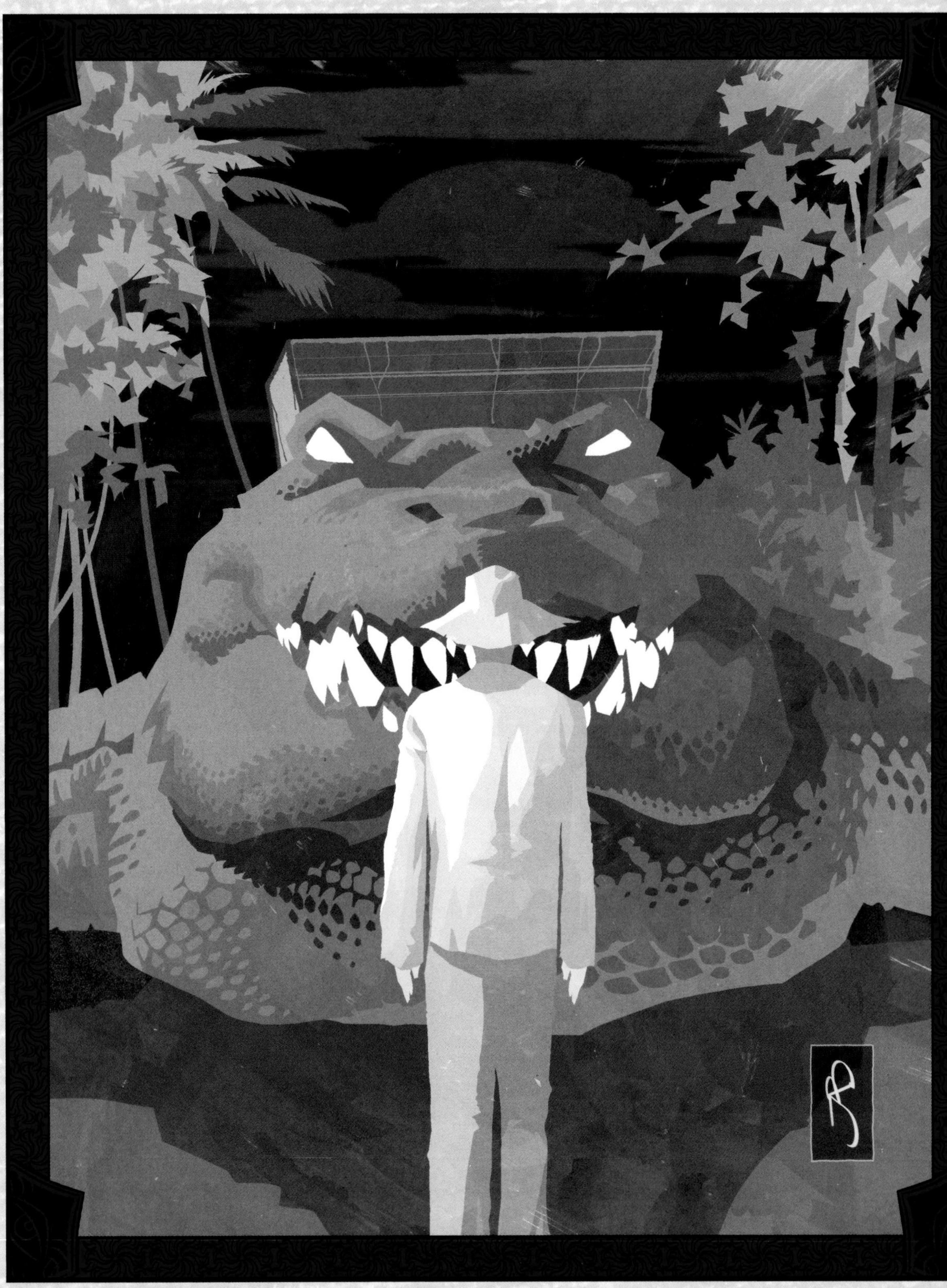

Based on the *Buwaya*'s words to Timoteo, I'm speculating that the Beast has entered a kind of mystical aestivation, "aestivation" being the reverse of hibernation.

It's when an ectotherm (an organism colloquially said to be "cold-blooded") enters a state of dormancy during hot, dry summers.

I think that during this mystical aestivation, the Beast is also undergoing something akin to parabiosis ("the anatomical joining of two individuals, especially artificially in physiological research" as per the Oxford English Dictionary), becoming this "new" and "terrible" thing, whatever that might prove to be.

(I'm fairly certain that Poltergeist also played a part in my dubbing it "the Beast".

The things pop culture leaves in your subconscious…)

The following, meanwhile, was laboriously recounted over a number of entries:

He was still a convalescing guest in Timoteo's home when Kolya witnessed what seems to be the initial phase of the *Buwaya* preventive help, though he is at first uncertain whether he actually witnessed the events he described, or if they were a particularly vivid dream.

He says he was awakened from sleep by the sound of Timoteo's chanting from outside.

Groggily, he walked to the window and saw that, impossibly, the spring had grown in its proportions, and it was now the size of a vast lake.

And not just any lake. It was, Kolya realized with a start, Lake Onega, the sight of which he had missed dearly.

Timoteo stood on the shore of Petrozavodsk Bay and emitted a sound at an "almost unbearably high pitch."

Soon afterwards, a *Buwaya* rises from the waters and emerges onto the shore.

At first, Kolya thinks the *Buwaya* has come for his friend, and he tries to speak, to perhaps try and convince his friend to stay, but, like the tongue of a crocodile, he finds his own suddenly unable to move as it usually does.

As a result, Kolya cannot speak, and can only watch as Timoteo approaches the *Buwaya*.

But Timoteo does not enter the "coffin" on its back. Instead, it is the *Buwaya* that moves, twisting its body, and very quickly and very savagely, bites its own tail off.

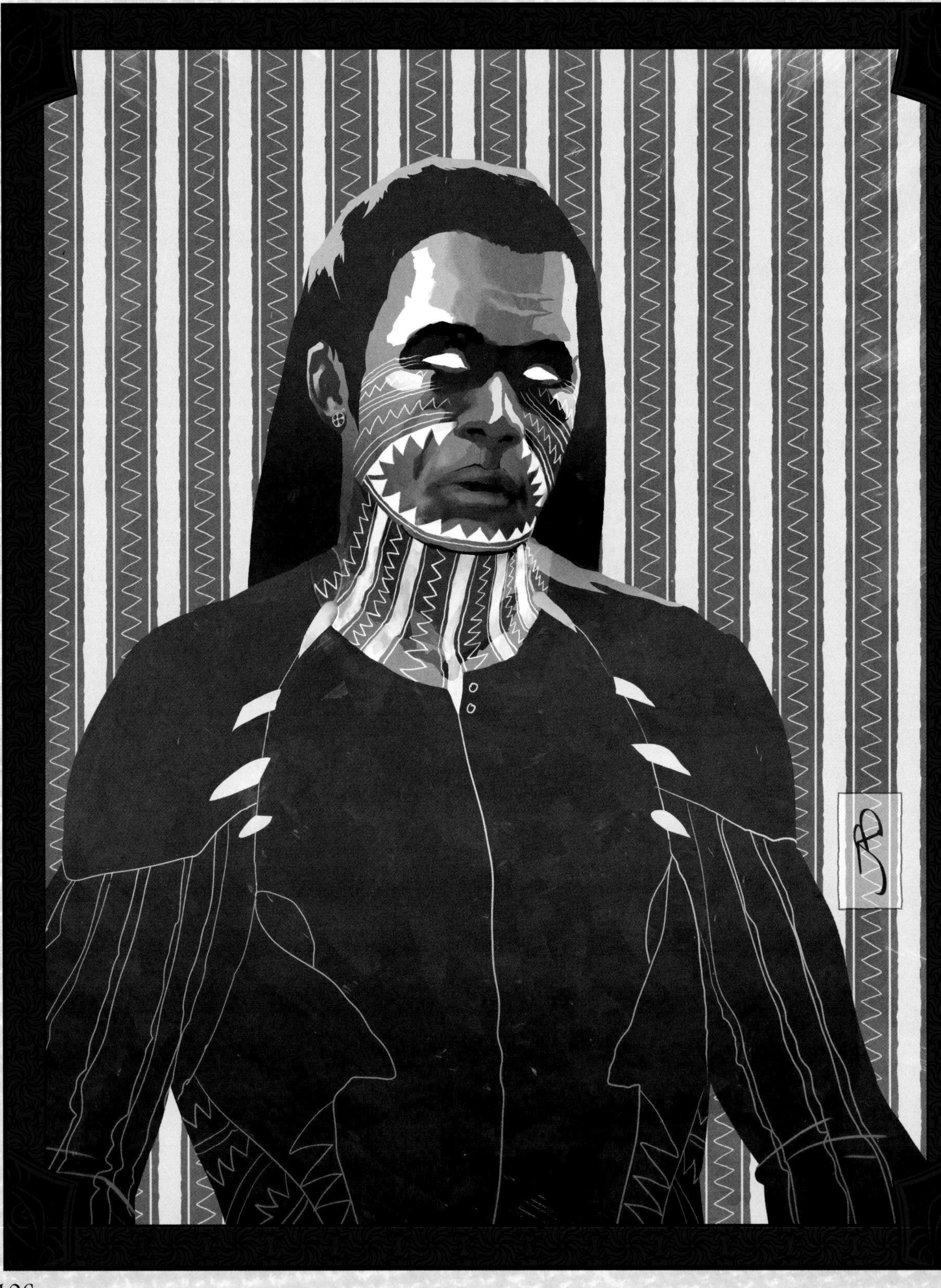

And while the shock of that sudden flurry of self-inflicted violence swamps Kolya, he sees that the *Buwaya* seems to spit out a number of its teeth onto the ground at Timoteo's feet.

Timoteo kneels before the *Buwaya*, then bends, forehead touching ground.

The *Buwaya* exhales, as if breathing some kind of benediction on Timoteo.

And then, suddenly, just for an instant, Timoteo is no longer bent down on the ground, he is standing, and *old*, white hair whipping in the wind.

It registers quickly that Kolya is no longer looking at Timoteo.

This is another man. An old man, dressed in sleeping garb, certainly nothing that can keep him warm in the cold.

Kolya sees that the gazes of the old man and the *Buwaya* are locked, as if they are one.

The old man is just about to take his first step towards the *Buwaya*, when the instant passes, and it is suddenly Timoteo there once more, bent down before the *Buwaya*.

Blessing given, the massive creature turns, and returns to the lake-that-is-supposed-to-be-a-spring.

The last thing Kolya recalls is seeing Timoteo on the shore, the *Buwaya*'s teeth and tail the only evidence the behemoth had ever been there.

Kolya awakens the next morning with Lake Onega gone, the spring back to its usual dimensions. He recounts his "dream" to Timoteo, and his friend smiles at him, saying he was "blessed" to have been a "witness."

When Kolya presses Timoteo for more, the *Manggagamot* simply smiles.

Kolya notes that it is an "odd" smile.

There is fondness and pride in the smile, but also a touch of sadness.

It is a month later, on the next new moon, that Kolya realizes that what he witnessed may very well have actually taken place.

By this time, he has fully recovered from the supposed "breakbone fever" and has returned to the *hacienda*.

He does, of course, still visit Timoteo and his father frequently, and it is on one such visit, on the night of the new moon, that he is introduced to Aiman, a friend of the *Manggagamot*.

Aiman is half-Filipino, half-Malay, and apparently a formidable warrior pledged to the *Buwaya*. He is tattooed, with "lines on the sides of his face that are meant to represent the jaws of the *Buwaya*."

He is also "taller and larger than any man I have seen in these islands, very nearly my size and bulk." Aiman is visiting to help Timoteo fashion weapons from "large specimens of bone and teeth."

Kolya is amazed and speechless when he is shown these items and looks agog at Timoteo, who merely smiles that same smile he did when Kolya recounted his "dream" to him.

Kolya, however, does not get to see what the weapons look like when they are completed, for upon his next visit, Aiman has already left, taking the weapons with him.

All Timoteo tells him are the weapons' names: *Ekor* and *Cakar*.

We will return to *Ekor* and *Cakar* (Malay for "tail" and "claws," respectively) in the next section.

Before we leave this particular matter for the time being, two things:

One — It should be noted that in both the PC and the latter portion of Kolya's journal, are entries relating sightings by the townsfolk of a "tailless *Buwaya*" in the river.

Kolya's entries which chronicle these sightings are of course, far more informed than Pardo's, who was apparently oblivious to Aiman's visit to Timoteo.

I can, in fact, find no mention whatsoever, however fleeting and cursory, of Aiman in the PC, and am open to the possibility that Pardo never met him at all, and never knew of his existence.

There were, it seems, many, *many* things that were going on right under the rigidly upheld nose of the one and only Alejandro Pardo.

Two — I am assuming that just like their crocodile "children," the *Buwaya* are also polyphyodonts, able to replace each tooth up to 50(!) times during their lifespan.

So, while that *Buwaya* may have been tailless, I'm willing to bet it had each and every one of its teeth intact.

Now, while there are still a host of entries in Kolya's journal that are worth mentioning, there are limits to the amount of space that the page count our publishers so generously offered us will allow.

So, while it's possible we will eventually be able to showcase those entries in a potential future volume, for now, we will need to push forward to the end of Kolya's journal.

Or rather, its non-end.

The Non-Ending of Kolya's Journal; or, An Appointment Fulfilled

Following that series of entries, the lives of Pardo and company once again return to their version of "normal."

Pardo does not make mention of the incident on the bridge ever again, or, if he did, either Kolya did not make an entry of it, which is doubtful, or it may have been recounted on one of the damaged pages.

A significant portion of the latter part of the journal (including its final pages) sustained particularly severe damage, so much so that there is no way to tell how the journal ended, or the manner in which the group disbanded, if that even happened before the journal ran out of pages to write on.

I assume the group disbanded because later entries in the PC seem to suggest that at a certain point, both Asif and Kolya were no longer in Pardo's company.

While we know that Kolya eventually returned to Russia, it is admittedly possible that Asif died during one of their adventures, thus explaining his later absence.

And while I wouldn't put it past Pardo to just not even mention a colleague's death, again, I doubt this is what happened, though in this case, I couldn't tell you why. It's a *feeling* I have.

Somehow, I just know that, like Kolya, Asif eventually left the Philippines, though as to where he went afterwards, we have no way of telling at the moment.

And, now that his journal had made me aware of the surname Kolya's family adopted when he left for the Philippines, I knew what to look for in the records.

And, true enough, when Kolya returned home, he took on that surname, shedding the one he'd used while traveling with Pardo.

Records show that at the ripe old age of 101, Kolya was last seen on the shores of Lake Onega, looking out towards Petrozavodsk Bay. This was in early November, just before winter would freeze the waters.

Though he was officially listed as "Missing," most everyone was of the mind that he'd simply grown tired of living and had swum out into the cold waters of the bay.

I, however, choose to believe that, had anyone happened to look towards Kolya—at that old man standing alone on the shore—at just the *right* moment, they would have been awed by the sight of a gargantuan crocodile emerging from the bay.

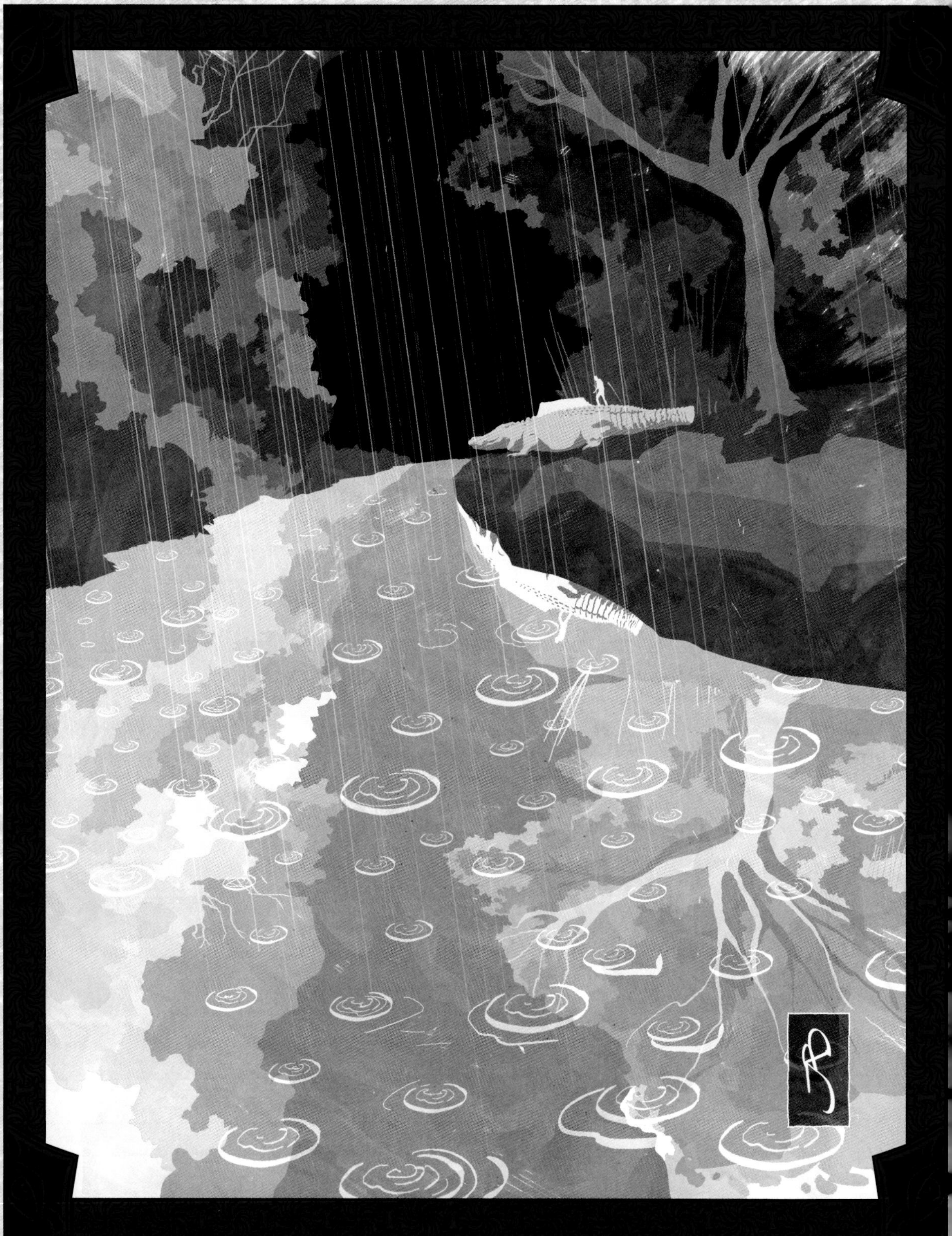

This crocodile would have been singular in its appearance, not only because of its size, but also because it had no tail.

They would have seen the old man walk calmly towards the behemoth, and step into a curious box-like growth on its back.

They would have watched as the tailless giant returned to the waters of the bay, and they would have wept for no reason they could articulate.

I choose to believe that the vision Kolya witnessed while recuperating in Timoteo's home, the vision Timoteo believes Kolya had been "blessed" to see, was a kind of premonition.

And a message, from the *Buwaya*. The setting down of an inevitable appointment.

And there, back home, at the end of his long and fruitful life (records also showed that he married a few years after returning from the Philippines, a union that produced seven children), the *Buwaya* had finally come to take Kolya on to his just rewards.

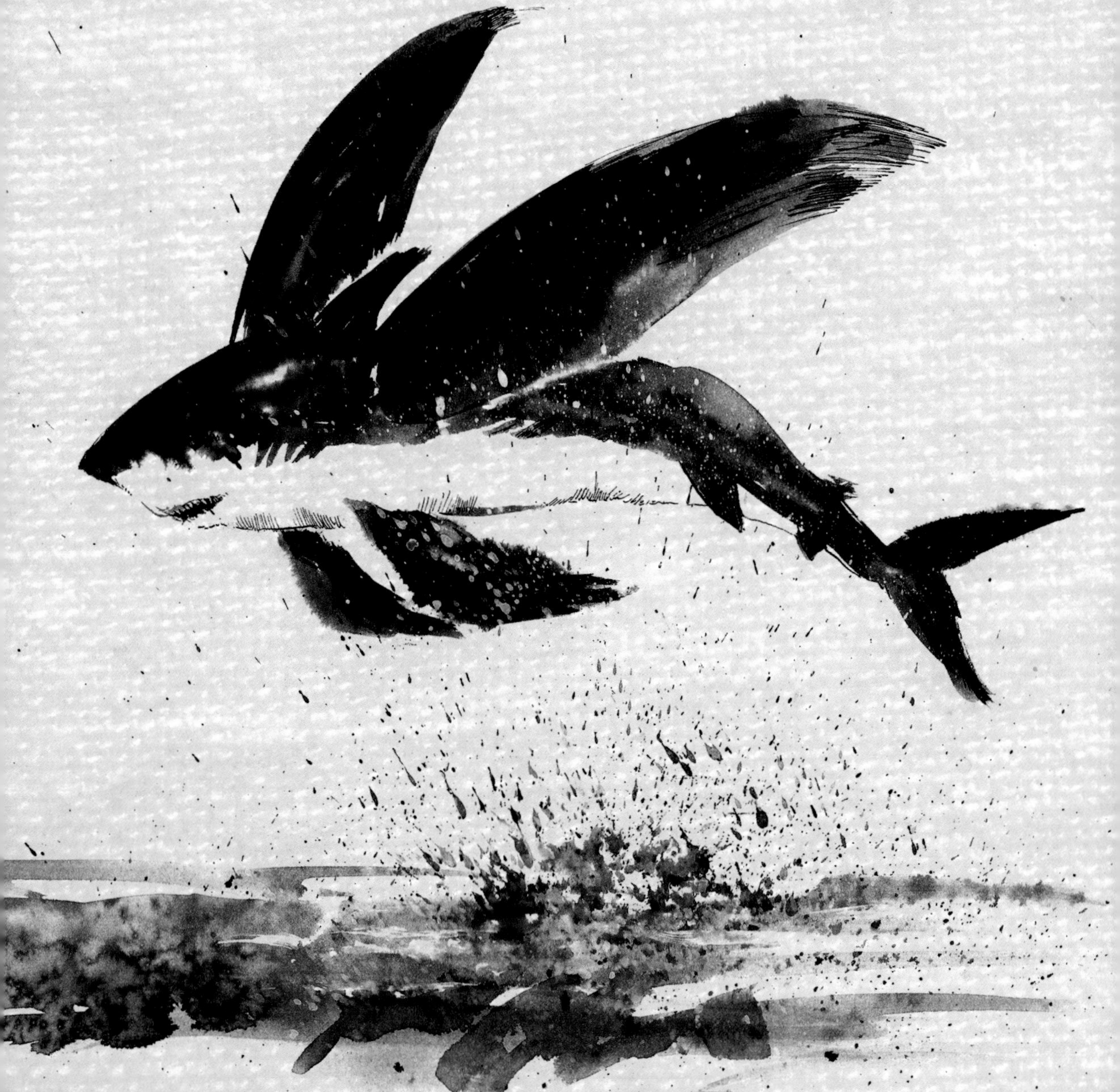

TIBURONES

One of the most feared creatures of the Visayan sea is the *Tiburones*. From a distance, people are confused on whether they are seeing a great white shark or a manta ray.

When it finally strikes, sailors and fishermen are shocked to see this 20-foot shark leap into the air, fly upwards, and then swoop down with its mighty manta-like wings to pluck them off their boat or ship.

In Bicol, they are known as the *Pating* na Pakpakan. The only written record of these flying beasts was in the Ibalon epic where the great hero Handyong supposedly tamed them. Many fishermen and ship captains have attempted to find a *Tiburones* that they can tame, thinking it would be a useful pet. Most times, they have returned empty-handed, never seeing even a fin or wing of the great predator.

The unlucky ones would never return to tell their tale.

It was on the sixth night that we were sailing along the San Bernardino Strait when we finally found the Tiburones. Well, it was more like it found us.

Despite all our preparation and thinking we had the upper hand, the entire crew was stunned to see the menacing creature catch the cannonball in mid-air and crush it with its dagger-like teeth.

I opened fired with my newly purchased musket, but the balls just bounced off the flying beast's grey hide.

It was finally driven away by my colleague's harpoon, which stabbed the beast's right eye. Of course, he was only able to do that because I had distracted it with my amazing marksmanship.

A. Pardo

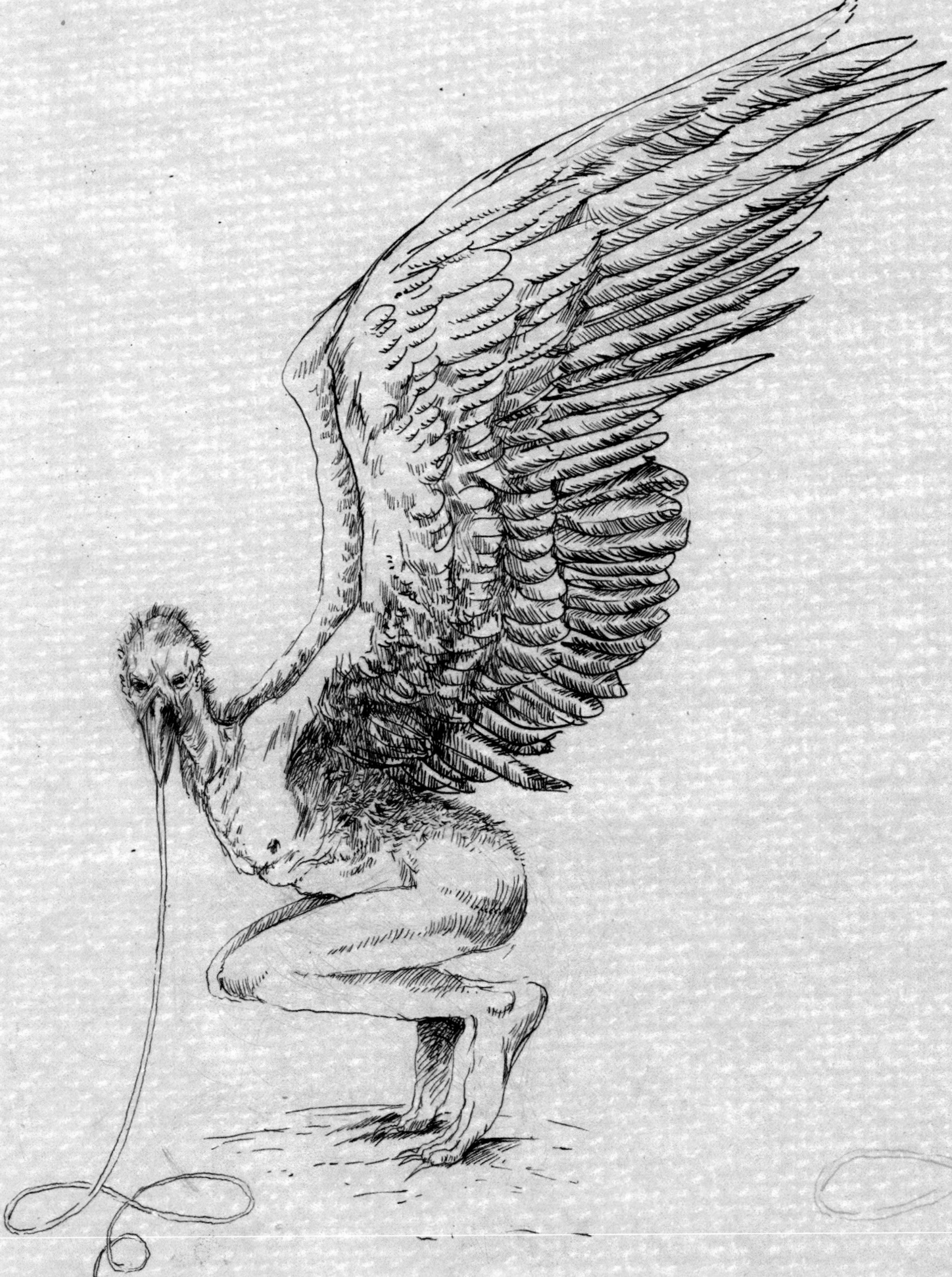

TIKTIK

The elders from Eastern Visayas say that if a pregnant woman wakes up in the middle of the night and hears a "tik tik tik tik" sound coming from outside the house, then it means the *Tiktik* is already inside her room.

This bird-like creature can somehow project its voice so that it will always sound like it is far away when it's already in striking distance of its prey. It would most probably be hanging upside down from the ceiling, where it would extend its long, snake-like tongue and use it to feed on the fetus of the pregnant woman.

The *Tiktik* can take on a human's appearance during daytime and interact with people in the village, looking for women who are several months pregnant.

At night, it would transform into its avian form, with its ebony feathers, razor sharp talons and prehensile tongue.

There have been reports that the *Tiktik* sometimes works with the *usang*, a kind of viscera sucker. The *Tiktik* would act as a scout, looking for infants, which is the favorite meal of the *usang*. The *usang* would then use its tongue to suck out the entrails of the child. In return, the *usang* informs the *Tiktik* of households with pregnant women.

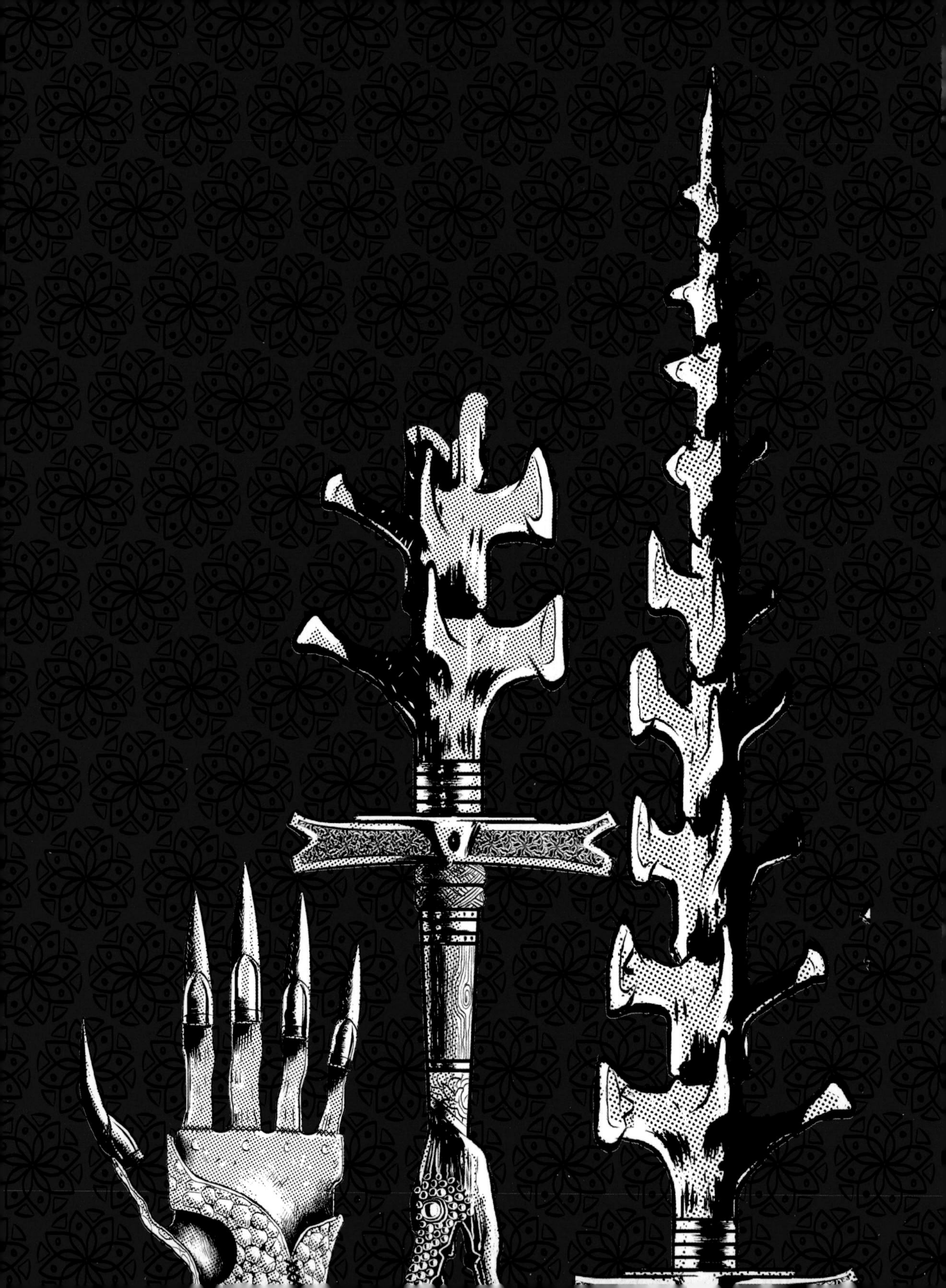

DEFENDING AGAINST THE DARK: CAKAR AND EKOR

If anyone would have told my Grade 5 self that I would one day be holding real magic weapons in my hands, I'd have told them, "*Now! Now!! NOW!!!*"

These aren't quite what I had in mind back then of course ("So this is a plus-what sword, exactly? And how many XP is it?"), but the goosebumps are undeniable.

In the palm of my left hand are (for lack of a better term) gloves, made from crocodile hide and brass, equipped with what appear to be large crocodile teeth on the fingers, so they look like—and can be used as—claws.

And I hold in my right hand (or rather, prop up, because it is heavy like you would not believe) a sword whose blade seems to be the tailbone of a massive crocodile.

Yes.

I am reasonably certain that I am in the presence of the weapons that were fashioned by Timoteo and Aiman, as per Kolya's journal entry.

These are *Cakar* and *Ekor*.

For a moment, I understand *exactly* what Stanislav feels when he gets excited at the prospect of a costume and a code name. I want to shout their names to the heavens, hoping some magic thunderbolt will energize me into the kind of warrior I know I'm not.

But that's not how this is going to work. At least not with me. (Again, the sword is heavy, not to mention the fact that my hands are too small for those gloves.)

Like I said: I know my limitations.

And though they may not exactly be magic weapons of the kind *Dungeons & Dragons* familiarized my younger geek self with, they're still weapons that were prepared to be used against the Beast, so, hey, that's "magic" to me.

Or rather, "magic" to whomever eventually wields them.

One of the interesting things about these weapons is that no one I've talked to seems to know where they came from. As far as they know, they've always been in the compound's arsenal.

Tests were run on them a few years back, and the results were curious, at least for some experts.

Judging from the size of the teeth used to make *Cakar*, these were teeth that came from the mouth of a *Deinosuchus*, or, at the very least, a closely related species (see *Buwaya* entry in LJ). But tests also showed that these teeth and bones did not show the right amount of aging for specimens from a long extinct animal.

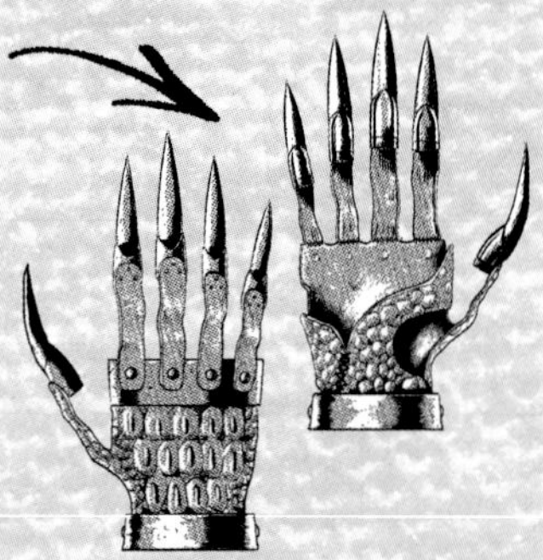

Test results showed that these teeth and bones dated to somewhere in the vicinity of the *first half of the 19th century*.

The tests also indicated that the work that turned them into weapons was also conducted in that same time frame.

No one can also seem to explain what method was used to make *Ekor*, to A) Get such a fine cutting edge from bone, which normally does not hold one. (Certain sections of the tail bone blade have noticeably been honed to a razor sharp edge.)

B) Fashion a blade from bone that not only shows no sign of breaking or flaking (as bone usually does), but is also apparently far more rigid than diamond.

The tests determined that the blade has a tensile modulus* of just a little over 2000 GPa (gigapascal). Diamond is rated at 1220 GPa, while tooth enamel (teeth are the hardest part of the human body) is 83 GPa.

So the tests were saying that these teeth and bones were taken from the animal while it was still alive, and then immediately made into weapons, using methods no one can fathom.

And all this happened sometime between 1801 and 1850.

These are the kinds of test results that, even when the numbers and the data are staring them right in the face, certain experts will still scoff at and ridicule.

It can be exasperating, trying to convince the majority that these things exist, and that many of them are not benign.

Meanwhile, since R.J. declared them not her "style," both Gus and Stanislav have been openly campaigning to be the official wielders of *Cakar* and *Ekor*.

Having seen the illustrations of Aiman in Kolya's journal, Gus is now seriously considering facial tattoos.

For his part, Stanislav had this to say: "Gus can have the Catwoman claws, but the sword is mine. I will be like He-Man, yes? By the power of... What is the name of this sword again? *Ee-kohr?*"

(Considering this was my thought exactly when I first saw *Ekor*, I suppose it just goes to prove that "geek" is a universal mindset, no matter what part of the world you're from.)

---

*Tensile (or Young's) modulus is defined as the measure of a material's stiffness or rigidity.

NOX TACTICAL
SYSTEMS
1.5 SECOND DELAY

MODEL 1882
FLASH BANG

AFTERWORD

With the deadline for this book's manuscript looming (I swear, I can actually hear the drumming of the publisher's fingers right now), I was toying with two ideas for this Afterword.

The first (and admittedly lazier option) was basically to echo the wrap-up of the LJ's Afterword.

To tell you, the readers, that there was still so much more (and there is, in the PC and Kolya's journal) that you needed to see.

That you deserved to see.

And that you could help us get the word out by, again, talking about this book.

The second idea was to underscore the tragic (and infuriating) irony that even though Kolya managed to protect his drawing hand during the santelmo experiment, I have the impression that the instance of automatic writing when he acted as a medium for the *Boroka* had an effect on his art.

It wasn't anything obvious, and in fact, Kolya never even mentions it in the surviving subsequent entries. He seems more concerned about having his penmanship return to normal.

But I noticed differences between the illustrations and sketches before that single Chavacano entry, and those that followed.

Again, nothing obvious, but there were differences, however slight (at least, as far as I could see, past all that unfortunate damage to the journal pages). As if his motor control over his drawing and writing hand was no longer as refined as it once was.

And this was still a direct result of Pardo's actions on the bridge.

But I was also going to attempt to balance that sentiment against the fact that Pardo did manage to help people, that he wasn't a complete blackguard.

(That wouldn't have been an easy task, but I would have tried.)

But I found that damned email in my Inbox, and now, with the deadline still looming (and the finger-drumming still audible), I really have no choice but to talk about that.

I've received word that my former colleague was found dead.

No details regarding cause of death have been released, and there doesn't seem to be an investigation forthcoming.

There was also, apparently, a very quick cremation arranged by his family.

If you'd ask me right now what I felt, I honestly wouldn't be able to tell you.

There's just the turbulence of emotion, so many feelings and thoughts, conflicting and clashing.

I'm a mess.

And yes, it's because I'm grieving. He was a close friend before he ever became a work colleague.

But the truth is, I lost him long before I read that email.

I lost him sometime during the process of getting the LJ published. I lost him when he *changed*. After that moment, I never really saw my old friend again.

What I'm about to say will undoubtedly rile his family, but I'm past caring about what they think, about their characterizations of me in interviews as someone who's "disturbed" and who "badly needs help."

What I'm about to say will make them think even worse of me.

This is what troubles me the most about this development.

I have no idea what the circumstances of his death were, nor the state of his body when it was found. And who did find it?

Was there even an autopsy before the quick cremation? Did someone actually take a close look at the body?

How do I know that wasn't just a banana trunk made to *look* like his body that they burned?

How do I know that he isn't still out there? Not my former colleague and friend, but whatever it is that took his place, whatever it is that changed him…

I'm aware I sound paranoid.

But you know what?

Paranoid is what's made it possible for me to still be here, writing this Afterword.

Paranoid is what's kept me from being *changed*, just like he was.

The world is now full of shadows for me.

Shadows where *anything* could be lurking, doing its best not to make any noise so as not to alert me to its presence.

Maybe the world was always like that.

But now, for better or worse, my eyes are open.

I hope we're helping open your eyes, too.

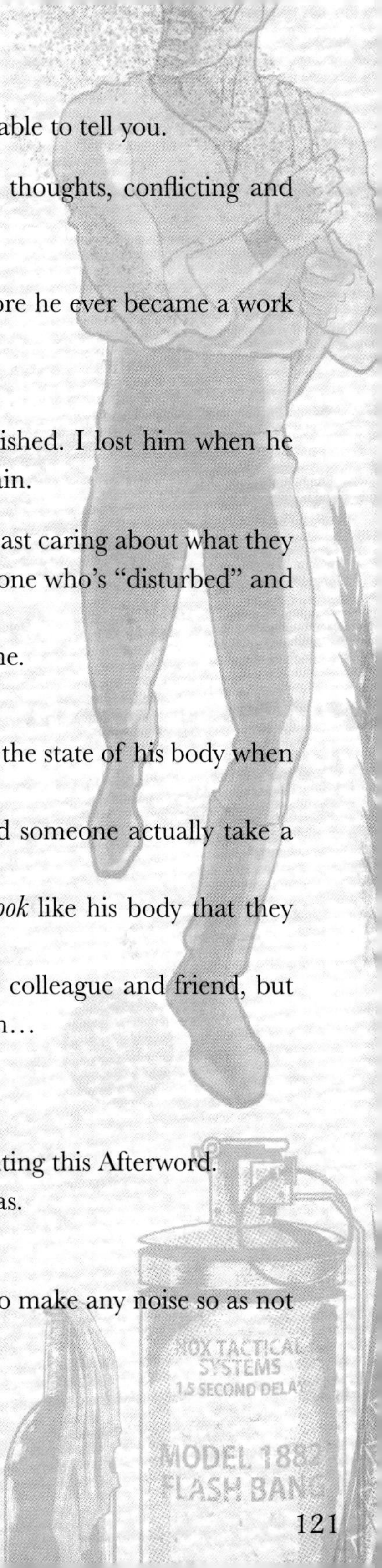
SYSTEMS

CREATORS' CATACOMB

David Hontiveros is the Palanca Award-winning and National Book Award-nominated writer of the horror/dark fantasy novellas *Craving, Parman*, and *Takod*, and the *Seroks* science fiction collections (*Iteration 1: Mirror Man* and *Iteration 2: Once in a Lifetime*). A sample of his short fiction (*Balat, Buwan, Ngalan*) can be found in the anthology *Alternative Alamat*. His short comic book work can be found in Summit Media's *Underpass* (*Judas Kiss* and *Katumbas*) and Graphic Classics. He is a founding member of Alamat Comics, to which he has contributed *Bathala: Apokalypsis* and the titles collectively known as *The 'Verse* (*Agyu, Dakila, Kadasig, Tatsulok*, and *Uriel*).

He has been observed wandering dusty library halls, feverishly whispering, "The owls are not what they seem."

You may read more of his babbling at: fiveleggediguana. blogspot.com

Budjette Tan is an ad man by day and a comic book man by night. He is the author of *Trese*, a series of urban fantasy graphic novels, co-created with Kajo Baldisimo. *Trese* won the Best Graphic Literature award at the 2010, 2012, and 2013 Philippine National Book Awards and is now an animated Netflix television series. In 2014, Budjette's comic book *Mikey Recio and The Secret of The Demon Dungeon*, co-created with Bow Guerro and JB Tapia, won the National Book Award. He is co-founder and editor-in-chief of Alamat Comics.

In 2015, he was spotted vandalizing the walls of a building. He claimed he was painting a teleportation sigil that would allow him to get to work on time.

Kajo Baldisimo is the co-creator and illustrator of the award-winning comic book series *Trese*. While his day job keeps him drawing storyboards for Manila's top TV commercial directors, the most exciting part of the day (or night) for Kajo is the time he can go back to drawing more comic book stories—or if he still finds time to play with his Transformers and Hot Toys collection. At night, his toys whisper to him secrets of the *Star Wars* movies.

Bow Guerrero is the artist and co-creator of the award-winning *Mikey Recio and The Secret of The Demon Dungeon*. Recently, he's been part of the artistic teams behind the *Alejandro Pardo* series and *Doorkeeper* graphic novel by Summit Books. When he's not drawing, he's usually seen lurking around old churches, forts, historic landmarks, museums, and art galleries—all in the name of visual research.

Mervin Malonzo wrote and drew the National Book Award-winning comic *Tabi Po*, which was made into a television series.. He also worked with writer Adam David on another title called *Ang Subersibo*, a comic adaptation of Rizal's *Noli Me Tángere* and *El Filibusterismo*. He graduated magna cum laude in UP Fine Arts.

Mervin has collaborated with authors like Eliza Victoria (*After Lambana*) and Adam David (*Shake, Rattle and Roll*). With his wife and friends he operates the indie publishing house Haliya. When he is not making comics, he is creating websites, animations, and illustrations for other people and entities. It is rumored that he created a painting that allows him to travel back in time.

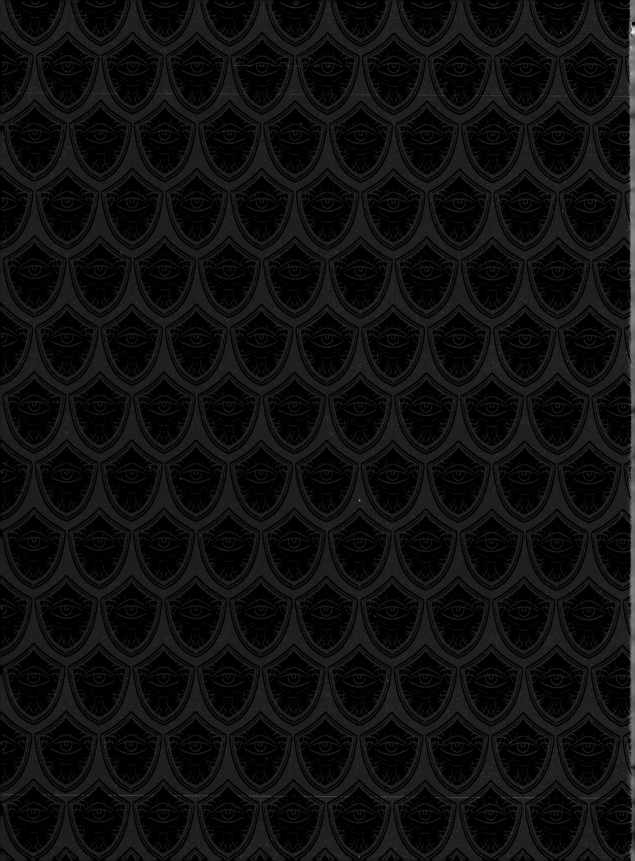

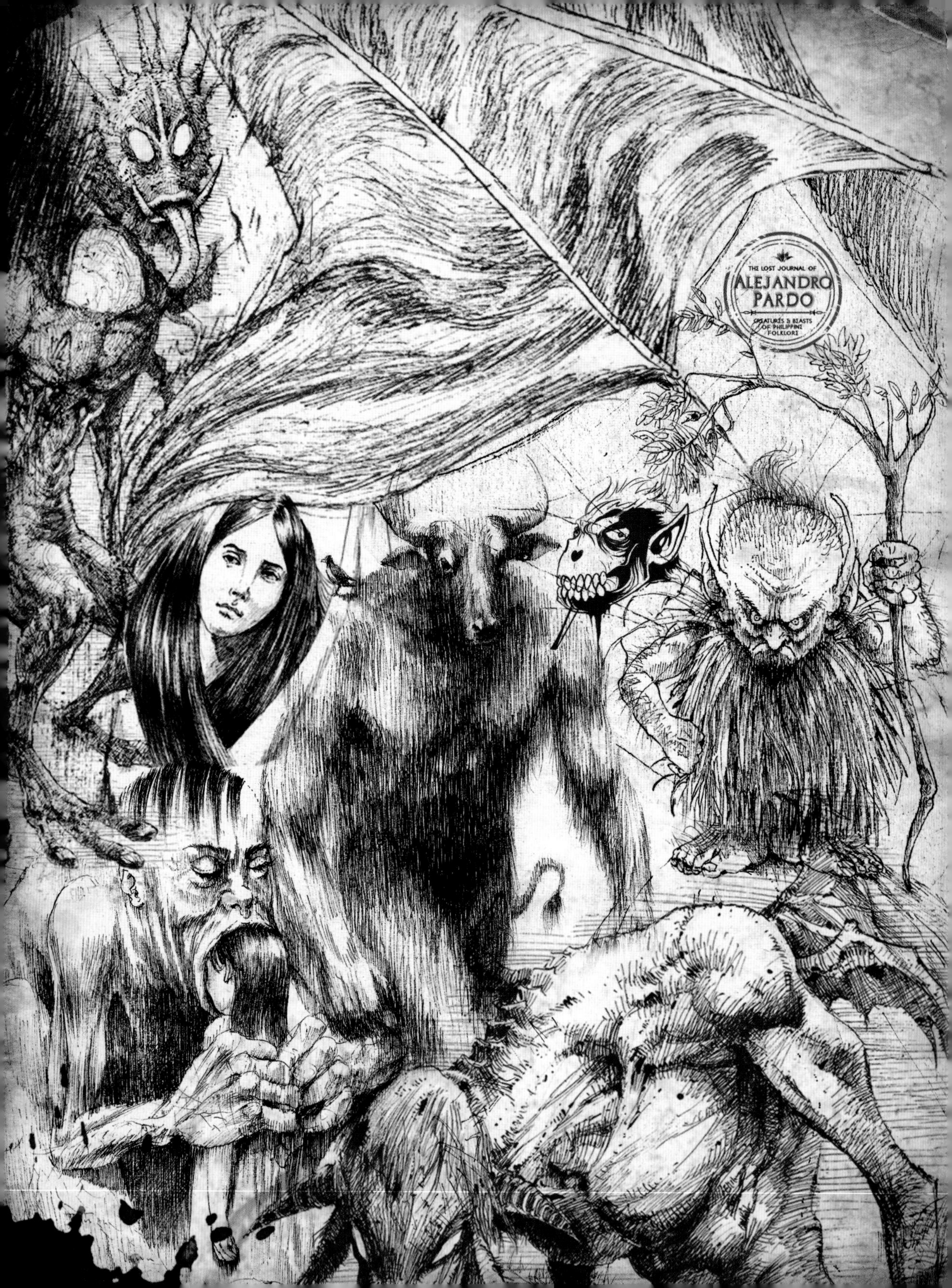
THE LOST JOURNAL OF
ALEJANDRO PARDO
CREATURES & BEASTS OF PHILIPPINE FOLKLORE

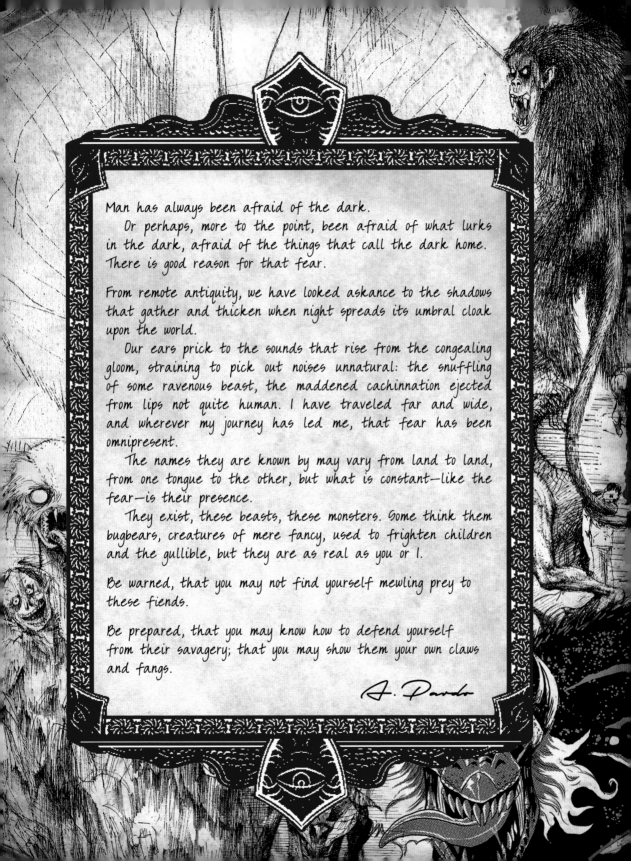

Man has always been afraid of the dark.

Or perhaps, more to the point, been afraid of what lurks in the dark, afraid of the things that call the dark home. There is good reason for that fear.

From remote antiquity, we have looked askance to the shadows that gather and thicken when night spreads its umbral cloak upon the world.

Our ears prick to the sounds that rise from the congealing gloom, straining to pick out noises unnatural: the snuffling of some ravenous beast, the maddened cachinnation ejected from lips not quite human. I have traveled far and wide, and wherever my journey has led me, that fear has been omnipresent.

The names they are known by may vary from land to land, from one tongue to the other, but what is constant—like the fear—is their presence.

They exist, these beasts, these monsters. Some think them bugbears, creatures of mere fancy, used to frighten children and the gullible, but they are as real as you or I.

Be warned, that you may not find yourself mewling prey to these fiends.

Be prepared, that you may know how to defend yourself from their savagery; that you may show them your own claws and fangs.

A. Pardo

"Books to Span the East and West"

Tuttle Publishing was founded in 1832 in the small New England town of Rutland, Vermont [USA]. Our core values remain as strong today as they were then—to publish best-in-class books which bring people together one page at a time. In 1948, we established a publishing office in Japan—and Tuttle is now a leader in publishing English-language books about the arts, languages and cultures of Asia. The world has become a much smaller place today and Asia's economic and cultural influence has grown. Yet the need for meaningful dialogue and information about this diverse region has never been greater. Over the past seven decades, Tuttle has published thousands of books on subjects ranging from martial arts and paper crafts to language learning and literature—and our talented authors, illustrators, designers and photographers have won many prestigious awards. We welcome you to explore the wealth of information available on Asia at **www.tuttle-publishing.com**.

Published by Tuttle Publishing, an imprint of Periplus Editions (HK) Ltd.

www.tuttlepublishing.com

Copyright © 2018, 2022 by David Hontiveros and Budjette Tan
Illustrations © 2018, 2022 by Kajo Baldisimo, Bow Guerrero and Mervin Malonzo
Book design by Frank Camara and Bow Guerrero
All rights reserved.

Library of Congress Control Number: 2022938486

ISBN 978-0-8048-5578-5

Published in the Philippines by Summit Publishing, 2018
First US edition, 2022

Distributed by

North America, Latin America & Europe
Tuttle Publishing
364 Innovation Drive
North Clarendon,
VT 05759-9436 U.S.A.
Tel: 1 (802) 773-8930
Fax: 1 (802) 773-6993
info@tuttlepublishing.com
www.tuttlepublishing.com

Japan
Tuttle Publishing
Yaekari Building, 3rd Floor,
5-4-12 Osaki, Shinagawa-ku,
Tokyo 141 0032
Tel: (81) 3 5437-0171
Fax: (81) 3 5437-0755
sales@tuttle.co.jp
www.tuttle.co.jp

Asia Pacific
Berkeley Books Pte. Ltd.
3 Kallang Sector #04-01
Singapore 349278
Tel: (65) 6741-2178
Fax: (65) 6741-2179
inquiries@periplus.com.sg
www.tuttlepublishing.com

26 25 24 23 22   5 4 3 2 1

Printed in China   2206EP

TUTTLE PUBLISHING® is a registered trademark of Tuttle Publishing, a division of Periplus Editions (HK) Ltd.